HER
SEXY
CHALLENGE

a Firefighters of Station 1 romantic comedy

HER
SEXY
CHALLENGE

a Firefighters of Station 1 romantic comedy

SARAH BALLANCE

Entangled Publishing, LLC
2614 South Timberline Road
Suite 109
Fort Collins, CO 80525
Visit our website at www.entangledpublishing.com.

Lovestruck is an imprint of Entangled Publishing, LLC.

Edited by Heather Howland
Cover design by Heather Howland
Cover art from iStock

Manufactured in the United States of America

First Edition August 2017

For Heather-from-Maine and her cohort The Albino, both of whom I'm told are the most awkward people to have ever stumbled through life. (And also a restaurant or two. Ahem.)

Chapter One

Caitlin Tyler adjusted her glasses and immediately regretted relinquishing her grip on the bridge railing that kept her from plunging to her watery demise. Despite the periodic blindness caused by her wind-whipped hair smacking her in the face, she already saw herself going over the edge, the dark swirling water below stealing her last sputtering breaths.

She'd seen rivers before. Near her home in rural Wyoming, every roadside dip and swale had a sign naming the river or creek it marked. Sometimes they even had water in them.

Sometimes they were raging torrents of death.

This river was creeping up on the latter, agonizingly reminiscent of the flash flood that tore unexpectedly over dusty ground and swept away her family's truck. She hadn't seen water churn like this since that night.

And the bridge…it was *really high* up.

Why had she thought she could do this?

Because most people can cross a bridge? She had crossed this very one the day before, in fact, only tucked safely within the confines of a bus.

She'd traveled light, planning to start her new life in Dry Rock, Colorado—which, with its roaring river, was decidedly *not* dry—as proprietor of Shelf Indulgence, a used book store wedged between an old-fashioned ice cream parlor and a candy store in the trendy downtown district. She'd thought the location perfect for a brick-and-mortar bookstore revival, if a bit tough on skinny jeans.

The potential for perfection was still there…if she ever managed to get to the other side of this godforsaken bridge. Maybe she could put a cot in the back of the store and survive on takeout?

She should have taken the bus again. Or a cab. Anything that would have involved being forced across the span, the river comfortably out of view. Instead, she'd decided to tackle it head-on, big girl panties hitched to her neck, pride higher than those not-so-distant mountaintops. She wasn't going to run away from her dream over a bunch of steel and concrete and a little bit of water.

Or so she'd told herself before she'd walked onto the bridge. Approximately halfway, she'd dared a peek down, and all of that flagging bravado took the plunge without her.

Ever since that moment, she'd had a death grip on the railing, her fingertips growing increasingly numb, every muscle fiber frozen by fear. Except her heart. Nope, that beat so hard the bridge shook.

The bridge *actually* shook.

Okay, so maybe giving up everything to run a bookstore in a random town she'd never heard of was crazy. She'd heard it a million times from just about everyone back home—her best friend, her mother, the postman, the guy who couldn't get her name right at the coffee shop. Even the neighbor's cat had tossed a haughty, accusing stare her way when she'd packed up the treat bowl she kept out for him.

But that hadn't deterred her. The cat could scowl all

he wanted, because she was going to take that English Lit degree—the one they'd all assured her would be useless in life—and put it to work.

At least, that had been the plan ten minutes ago.

Now, she was almost certain she wouldn't live long enough to hear everyone gloat. Which, come to think of it, might be an upside. One that didn't make it any more comforting to find herself clinging to the cross-town bridge, life flashing before her eyes while a deluge of regrets flew past at a speed that far outpaced the steady, pavement-shaking pace of what had to be every vehicle within a thirty-mile vicinity.

She gnawed on the inside of her cheek, too tense and terrified to bite her nails or do anything that would ever, ever require her to let go again.

Passing cars churned exhaust in her face, sending road grit pinging against her legs. She tried to take a deep, steadying breath, but all she inhaled was road dust. She coughed, almost losing her grip and her glasses over the course of a single spasm.

Distant sirens cut through the shuffle of the traffic.

Before she could process what that meant, a motorcycle passed too closely, and she let out a high-pitched scream. A trio of big ugly birds that had been perched just a few feet away, staring down their hooked beaks at her, launched skyward. Another semi-truck roared by, sending a few brute tons of steel and concrete swaying beneath her feet.

"Nope, nope, nope." Steel and concrete were *not* supposed to move.

A gust of wind rocked her, almost sending her glasses into the river again. She managed to smash them back against her face without fully losing her grip on the railing, though an unexpected draft suggested her skirt might have fluttered indecently around her thighs. Great.

The sirens grew louder.

Oh God. She *literally* couldn't breathe. Her throat felt like a clogged vacuum hose, and the harder she fought for air, the more the world seemed to blur and spin around her. Hugging the railing felt like the worst idea in the world, but it was the only solid thing within her reach. Desperate not to fall into traffic, she edged closer to the barrier, almost grateful for the sparkly edges of her vision that kept her from seeing the rushing water.

The last time she'd seen rushing water, she'd nearly lost everyone she loved.

Her teeth started to chatter.

No one slowed to check out the woman frozen mid-span. Apparently, pedestrians hung out on this bridge on a regular basis.

They could have it.

If she made it off that death span alive, damned if she'd ever touch toe to it again.

• • •

Lieutenant Shane Hendricks assessed the scene before him. The call had been for a jumper, and sure enough, a woman clung to the railing halfway across the span. Traffic ahead had slowed to a static crawl, which meant the wind whipping that mess of red hair had to come from the water. She didn't look in imminent danger of going over, but he wasn't one to take chances.

He radioed down to make sure the rescue boat was in place. Not a stretch there…after years of calls like these, the vessel docked near the pilings, but he received confirmation they were ready. The ambulance waited at the foot of the bridge, ready to maneuver in either direction.

Just another day at the office.

He didn't know what it was about this span, but at least

once a month since he'd signed on with the department nearly ten years ago, they had someone threatening to go over the side. Those who had followed through tended to be thrill seekers in their teens and early twenties looking for a good time, and most walked away unscathed.

People who wanted to jump just did it.

In his experience, people who made a huge spectacle—like the woman in question—rarely wanted more than attention. And they got it after effectively shutting down the only bridge between the suburban sprawl of Dry Rock and the downtown area, which was wedged between the mountains and the river. Almost everyone had to cross that river to get to work or shop or actually *do* anything, and even then, the pickings were fairly light. Dry Rock only pretended to be a city.

He hated it.

It was an odd place to be, knowing he helped people, but feeling like he would never measure up to what he wanted from his career as long as he was stuck there. Fighting fires, outsmarting and outmaneuvering nature, was in his blood. He needed high rises and an urban hardscape—a place where they really needed him. Somewhere he could make a real difference, like his dad had.

His father had died a hero.

In Dry Rock, Shane helped cats out of trees and talked people off bridges. It wasn't the most heroic of jobs, though that woman, who seemed to be alternately crying and talking to herself, might pose a bigger challenge than most.

Two weeks. That's all he had left in this town. He'd accepted a job in Denver, fighting *real* fires. Continuing his father's legacy in the city that had taken him. Going back would break his mother's heart, but he had to go.

He was meant for it.

"What do you think, Lieutenant?" Matt Freeman was

Shane's closest friend, but on a call, they kept things formal. That didn't stop Matt from filling Shane's truck with ping-pong balls when their shift ended, nor did it stop Shane from kicking his ass in retaliation, but there was a line.

On the job, they had the routine down.

Routine. Dry Rock in a nutshell.

Shane sighed and kept his eyes on the woman. Peripherally, flashes of red faded from traffic that had continued ahead while Matt brought the engine to a stop. Behind them, all lanes were blocked. "I need to get the hell out of this town."

Matt's soft laughter carried across the cab. "Before or after that woman does or does not jump?"

"She's not going to jump. She'd need a step ladder to get over the edge." Shane wasn't exaggerating by much, if at all. The pedestrian railing was more than half her height. Throwing herself over would prove a challenge, and the neon-white of her grip on the rail suggested she wasn't going anywhere any time soon.

He hopped off the truck, hitting the ground heavily in the turnout gear. He added the requisite helmet, kicking back the visor, and nodded to Matt. Show time.

The woman barely glanced his way as he approached. He wished he could get a better idea of her expression, but with a mess of red hair whipping into a tornado from the updraft, all he could tell was that her face had momentarily shifted in his direction, then back to the pavement.

His guys stopped traffic behind him, and by now the cars ahead had cleared the bridge. Red and blue lights flashed on the opposite side, suggesting the police had a barricade in place. The typically busy crossing had settled into an unnatural silence, over which he could hear stifled sobs that made whatever she mumbled between them indecipherable.

"Mind if we talk?" Shane asked the woman when he was close enough to be heard without yelling. The distance between them narrowed from twenty feet to fifteen before he eased his approach. He took in her cute, if prim, skirt and a blouse he was sure his grandma had owned back in the day and, weighing that with a set of healthy curves he probably shouldn't have noticed, decided she probably wasn't strung out on anything.

She looked at him in the same instant the wind died. Five seconds without her hair flying left him gut-punched. She was a redhead, all right, with killer green eyes. What he assumed to be mascara had fled the scene, having run to her neck in smears that stood vivid against her porcelain skin. Those same tracks had uncovered a smattering of freckles, and her tear-streaked face left her glasses without traction. He hadn't even noticed them, clunky and retro, until that moment when she pushed them against her face, which really said something about the intensity of that shade of green.

"Do I *look* like I'm standing here waiting for a sweaty fireman to come by and engage me in conversation?" she asked, sounding…annoyed, if shaky.

Huh. He'd never gotten that reaction before. And *sweaty*? He might have been buried under a few pounds of gear, but the morning temps still hovered in the sixties, the air cool against his face. "We don't have to talk. I'm here for whatever you might need."

"That sounds like a line from a bad date."

Some of the color came back to her knuckles. Either she was about to start climbing the fence, or her strange irritation over his presence made her forget whatever else had her clinging to the side of a bridge. When she didn't make for the railing, he bet on the latter.

"Pretty sure I've never been a bad date, so I wouldn't know," he said cautiously, watching her body language. Sure enough, her grip loosened, and she actually turned away from the railing instead of just twisting to look at him.

Bingo.

Her eyes flashed. "You just happened by to talk about your dating situation?"

He'd managed to knock the distance between them to about five feet, and she hadn't reacted to his proximity. Nor was she clinging to the bridge. He hitched an eyebrow and prayed he hadn't misjudged her. "Do you *want* to talk about my dating situation?"

He tried not to notice the way the morning sun set fire to her hair, or how those eyes reminded him of hiking in the spring when the evergreens sported new growth. He tried, and failed, which made her combative tone almost welcomed.

Almost. Because he still had a job to do.

"Yes," she said, like he'd asked the dumbest possible question. "That's exactly what I wanted from this day. Right after I found myself stuck on this bridge, I thought, I need a guy to come talk to me about his dating situation."

A grin tipped his mouth before he could stop it. He recognized the fear in her tone. Found her eyes swimming in it, but if turning fear into irritation toward him helped get her off this bridge the safe way, that was fine with him.

He was grateful Matt and the rest of his guys were at his back so as not to witness his facade splinter. Not that it was one. He was just doing his job, and if that meant goading her away from the edge, so be it. "Better me than the guy down there on the rescue boat. His dating situation isn't one for polite conversation, not that that stops him from oversharing."

Her eyes narrowed, then widened. She looked from him toward the direction of the fire truck, then toward the cops on the other end of the bridge, then back to him. "Wait. You think I'm going to *jump*?" Incredulity shook her small, curvy frame, and he noticed in every *possible* wrong way.

"Ma'am—"

Eyes lit, she launched on the offensive. "I don't want to

be *on* the bridge. Do you really think I want to be *under* it?"

He studied her a moment, momentarily lost by the way the wind outlined her body through her clothes. Gawked was more like it. It was inappropriate and unprofessional, but damn, he wished he'd run into her at the diner instead. Or at the grocery store. Anywhere else, because under any other circumstances, he could think of a hell of a lot more interesting things for her to be under than the bridge.

To her question, he replied, "Well, ma'am, whether you ended up under the bridge would depend on the direction of the current."

Her jaw dropped, then snapped shut. "Is *that* what you say to people who are about to jump?"

He kept his lips tight to hide another smile. "I thought you weren't jumping."

He was close enough now to invade her personal space. He could have easily grabbed her, but he didn't see any signs that she was about to go over the side, nor was there an obviously abandoned vehicle nearby. He couldn't imagine anyone taking the route by foot if they were afraid enough to freeze up, but this was Dry Rock. If she didn't have a ride, she might not have had a choice about walking across the bridge.

The irritation twisting her expression did nothing to kill his gnawing—and yep, still inappropriate—attraction. "I'm not jumping," she said, "so you can call off the fire trucks and the police cars."

"And the boat. And there's an ambulance, too." He moved closer, and she reclaimed every inch he gained, shuffling backward, her hand only lightly touching the railing. She probably hadn't noticed her own retreat.

"Please tell me you're kidding. There's really a boat?" She turned her head a fraction, then seemed to catch herself and jerked back toward him. The lull in momentum nearly had him tripping over himself not to walk right into her, though he wouldn't harbor too many regrets. Not with a growing interest in this woman—one that turned more into an ache with every step away from emergency response territory. He tried to shake it. The last thing he wanted was an entanglement in Dry Rock. Not with everything he wanted waiting just two weeks away in Denver. He'd have plenty of time to twist a few bed sheets there.

Off the clock.

"We care about our citizens," he said mildly. "That's why we have this great big high bridge to keep you away from that little stream."

"*Little stream?*" Horror blanched her face, and she took a few more steps back. "It looks like a dam broke down there."

He glanced over the side and continued his forward press. "Nope, it's calm today. You must not be from around here. It's almost impossible to live here and not cross this bridge, and I don't believe we've met."

He'd remember if they had. Now that they were off the middle of the bridge, her hair had quit whipping all over the place. A light breeze lifted the strands, and those glasses he'd thought clunky with their dark frames now seemed almost cute. She definitely had the librarian thing going for her, but the rest of the package was far from that of the dowdy old woman who'd policed the school's books when he was a kid. That woman had been about a hundred years old, tall and thin with the requisite bun. If Bridge Woman wore a bun, it would be the messy kind with a pencil stuck through it, the ends of her hair splayed like fire. Or a mad chicken.

That last thought made him grin.

Dropping his gaze to the rest of her wiped that smirk right off his face.

Everything suggested when the breeze had plastered clothing against her had been spot on. She was *hot*. Her button-up shirt gaped a bit unnaturally, exposing a nicely filled lacy black bra. Her skirt was probably knee-length but fluttered mid-thigh in the breeze as she continued to shuffle backward, revealing great legs. She wasn't stick thin. Just soft, curvy, and a good foot shorter than his six-plus-feet.

He couldn't remember such a flailing instant attraction to any woman, ever. The entire city of Denver could burn to the ground and the level of heat generated still wouldn't touch her, and damned if he didn't want to get his hands on her body.

One way or another, the next two weeks were going to be the longest of his life.

Second only to the next few moments. Because when she finally ran out of railing and the walkway made its subtle shift from bridge strata to plain old sidewalk, she didn't express an ounce of relief.

Instead, she wore a fierce scowl that suggested she wanted him dead, and she might get her wish if he spent one more second drowning in those spitfire green eyes. Holding tight to that ounce of self-preservation, he smiled and asked, "Now that you've been properly rescued from that big scary bridge, is there anything else I can do for you?"

He figured he'd goad her one last time, but the move backfired. Yeah, she glowered fury, but he'd overshot by a mile. He'd managed to push her buttons, but he'd also done a number on his own.

Because she couldn't be any less convenient, much less impressed by him.

And he couldn't remember ever wanting anyone more.

Chapter Two

Caitlin glared at the egotistical jerk with his stereotypical hero-complex, smirking at her because she'd been scared by a bridge.

Okay, so maybe his little trick deserved a smirk, but he was a first responder. Weren't they supposed to be above reproach and maybe *not* staring at her boobs?

He might rank as some kind of wizard for his ability to get her off that death span without her realizing it, but that didn't earn him the right to ogle her. Not even with those amazing whatever-color-they-were eyes. She bounced back and forth between hazel and chocolate before realizing she really didn't—*shouldn't*—care, and then wanted to kick herself for getting lost in his irises. But she could only see so much square jaw with the helmet in place, and height and broad shoulders meant nothing to a girl who couldn't get onto a barstool without a boost. In short, he had nothing to offer her, so her rampaging ovaries could shut the hell up.

Or at least find someone who hadn't enjoyed a front row seat to the most embarrassing moment of her life. "I'm fine," she said, lifting her chin. "Thanks for your help."

Maybe he'd go away and take his entire fleet of flashing lights with him. Now that she wasn't in danger of falling in and drowning, she dared a look at the river. Yep, lights on the boat, too. And a crowd had gathered, some watching and holding up phones—*great*—with the rest staring at their devices in their hands, probably telling the whole world what they'd witnessed. Traffic jammed the business district behind the lane closures, and she imagined the other side looked the same. A couple of blocks down, she could just see the signage hanging from the tavern-style wrought iron arm that poked from the front of her bookstore.

If she could only get there and hide.

It was all she could think of.

Behind the smirking firefighter, an ambulance eased toward them. It, too, blasted light, but at least the siren remained silent. She didn't need a ride—if anything, she needed to kick Mr. Hot and Bothering Her in the shin—but if she left in the ambulance, at least no one would see her walk directly to her store. Maybe she could avoid being *that woman* for a few more minutes, as if anyone could outrun the gossip of a thousand flashing lights and the dead stop of morning traffic.

Her fresh start was suddenly about as palatable as a gulp of lumpy milk.

Captain Ego glanced toward the guy who hopped from the ambulance parked a few feet away.

"Everything okay, Lieutenant?" the guy asked.

Okay, so *Lieutenant* Ego. She stood corrected. And she didn't need him to answer for her. "I'm fine," she said. "I had a moment on the bridge. It's over."

Ambulance Guy's brow rose. "If you need resources—"

"I'll make sure she knows who to talk to," Lieutenant Ego cut in.

She hated both their pitying tones. Hands on hips, she fired back, "I don't need resources. I'm afraid of the water. Deep, swirling, suck-you-under-until-you-die water."

Both men stared.

Oops. She hadn't planned on including the confession, and that left her flustered and seriously considering making a break for the mountains that backlit the city. Morning sun still dusted the peaks, where she knew, geographically speaking, there probably weren't raging rivers. Even the mighty Colorado started as droplets up there. She could handle that. No flash floods, no terrifying moments trapped with her family in a truck swept away by dark churning water.

Nope. Not thinking about that.

The men exchanged glances like she'd just admitted to never having bathed. Lieutenant Ego was the one to speak. "There's no water up here, ma'am."

His voice sounded funny, like he was trying to choke back laughter.

"I'm afraid of the water *under* the bridge," she clarified. And also heights, apparently, but no need to give them anything else to ridicule. "Either way, not going over the side, so you can stand down. With my thanks and apologies for disrupting your morning."

"Yes ma'am," Ambulance Guy finally said, backing off with a nod. But not before his eyes cut briefly, blatantly to her chest.

What was *with* this place? She scowled.

"You missed a button," Lieutenant Ego offered helpfully.

She looked down at her shirt, saw the gaping hole, and snatched the fabric back together. "I appreciate your concern," she said through her teeth. "If we could all go our separate ways now, that would be great."

Ego Man reached into his jacket to dig through his pockets, shoving aside enough of the heavy gear to reveal some serious heat beneath those layers. Flat abs and a chest that strained at the dark blue T-shirt he wore underneath.

Annoyed, she blew at the hair that whipped her face. *Double standards much?* But that wasn't even the problem. The problem was the surge of attraction that hit, and he was so not her type. Not that she had much of one. Her singular goal in dating was to avoid the overbearing men she seemed to attract back home. Showing up in a new town for a fresh start only to have her loins swoon over Mr. Overbearing himself was failure personified.

He removed his helmet and handed her the card he'd retrieved from his jacket. *Lt. Shane Hendricks.* Her fingers tingled where they'd brushed against his. "9-1-1 won't do the trick?" she asked.

His gaze tipped lazily from where he'd zeroed in on that tremble of her hand—surely he hadn't missed *that*—to her eyes. "This way's a bit more direct and won't bring the city to a grinding halt."

She legitimately blushed when he uttered the word *grinding.* Probably innocently—maybe not—but regardless of how he meant it, her face blazed red with her interpretation. The hitch in his smile suggested he noticed. His eyes seemed darker now, a shade richer than her favorite mocha. Her knees actually weakened, like she was some dopey teenager and not a grown-ass woman.

One who needed a lieutenant in a shining fire truck to get her off a bridge.

With the entire city to witness it.

But it wasn't the city that bothered her. It was a certain sex-on-a-stick firefighter who had the nerve to undress her with her eyes.

And her own traitorous body for responding.

Chapter Three

Caitlin's resolve to leave town disintegrated the moment she stepped into Shelf Indulgence, a century-old mainstay of Dry Rock, at least until its closure three years prior. Other than a renaming, the store hadn't been updated in decades, and she figured several of the ubiquitous dust colonies had to be older than she was. Still, there was nothing like the smell of old books, and the rows of library-like stacks fulfilled the geekiest girlhood fantasy ever had by anyone. It was her dream. She'd made it.

Twenty-five years old and nothing left to accomplish.

Except learn to cross a bridge so she could actually get to work.

But, bridge issue aside, life was good. She had her own bookstore filled with hundreds of volumes of utterly miscellaneous, uncatalogued tomes. Everything had come with the store, right down to the old-fashioned thumbtack cash register. It was as if a slice of history had just become hers, like she'd stepped back a few generations in time and had just acquired everything wonderful about the world. So what if it was positioned just a tiny bit too close to a raging river and a too-hot-for-his-own-good lieutenant? Compared to her hometown, Dry Rock was huge. Odds were good she'd never again have to look into those gorgeous brown eyes.

After one *Sound of Music*-esque twirl in the space made quirky by a vintage sofa and patchy mix-textured area rug that didn't match itself, much less anything else in the room, she had all the determination in the world to conquer that bridge.

And also to forget the man.

Despite her vow to banish him from her thoughts, an involuntary shiver chilled her skin. Guys like him had an entire card catalog full of feminine options hanging on his every word, though. No way was she his type. Intelligence ranked way lower than long legs and cups that runneth over. She wouldn't trade a single brain cell for a killer body, but that didn't mean she'd set herself up for a fall.

But that was all outside and long behind her. Within these walls, she had everything she could ask for, including a fully stocked coffee bar. The previous owners were an elderly couple who hadn't ventured beyond the traditional carafe of Columbian beans, so she'd treated herself by shipping ahead a Keurig and an assortment of K-Cups, and the delivery had been waiting on the front step for her when she'd arrived.

Everything was just about perfect, right down to the days of inventory she had ahead of her. The books with a UPC she could scan to add to her list. The rest, along with all of the organization, would probably take days to catalog.

A few hours and a couple cups of coffee later, the heat and dust were getting to her, and she'd only begun to dent the first of a dozen boxes of unsorted books. Plus, she'd missed lunch. She stepped out of the store long enough to grab a sandwich from the deli a couple of storefronts down from hers, and took a moment to appreciate the fresh mountain air. It seemed so clean, but then again, it didn't bear the dust kicked up by thousands of head of cattle back home.

Back at her store, all thoughts of clean air fled with a blast of stifled, furnace-like heat. She'd only closed up the place for thirty minutes or so, but the sun beamed through the windows, making it stifling. She eyeballed the window-unit air conditioner. She hadn't tried it, but it was clean, right down to the filter that popped out of the front, so she hit the button.

Room-temperature air surged from the machine. It almost immediately began to cool, and within a minute, genuinely frigid air blasted into the store.

Stupendously satisfied with her ability to press the power button, she headed back to her boxes of books.

She'd only scanned a few before an odd smell hit. She sniffed the book in her hand. Musty, yes, but not…smoke? Possibly the book had come from the home of a smoker, but the scent grew more pronounced by the moment, which didn't make sense for the book in her hand. She inhaled again, deeper this time, and almost choked from fear. Actual smoke.

Fire.

In her bookstore.

Her dream literally going up in smoke. No amount of insurance would fix that. She scrambled to her feet, knocking the books in her lap to the ground. "I'm sorry," she mumbled, fumbling for her phone. Apologizing to books.

Books that were about to die in a fire.

The smoke wasn't terrible, but it grew in intensity. She covered her nose and mouth and stumbled in the direction it seemed thickest. Seeing nothing, she backed away as she dialed 911, and by some miracle remembered the address of the store…well, right after she accidentally gave her home address. The old one in Wyoming.

At this rate, she wouldn't have to worry about slinking out of Dry Rock. They'd run her out.

She finished up with dispatch, muttering an agreement to the man's urge for her to vacate the premises and wait a safe distance outside. The smoke hadn't gotten much worse from the start of her call, but the entire building was full of tinder, so that could change in an instant. She'd seen a fire extinguisher, but where? *Bathroom*. Because the room with the water in it was precisely where it would be most needed. She skidded around the shelves, still on the lookout for flames, and was promptly hit with a cloud of smoke that had funneled between the stacks. Gasping, she forged ahead, managing to grab the extinguisher, then spun.

And hesitated.

She had to put out the fire.

But…*fire*.

But her books. Her store. The place was a historical landmark, for God's sake.

She had to save her books.

Smoke tumbled from the front half of the building. She glanced behind her. The back exit was completely clear. The view toward the ceiling had grown hazy, but she didn't see flames.

She hoisted the fire extinguisher and took careful steps toward the thickest smoke at front of the store…at which point the door flew open. Shocked, she squeezed the handle on the extinguisher, accidentally aiming it at the firefighter who burst through the entry, covering him in white powder.

He stopped in his tracks.

So did she. At least until he surged forward, strong arms grasping her and literally sweeping her off her feet as he "escorted" her to the back of the building, through the straight shot to the back exit. As soon as they were outside, he yanked off his helmet and breathing apparatus, revealing her worst nightmare.

Lieutenant Ego.

Flipping perfect.

"You could have been *killed*," he all but shouted.

"The fire," she sputtered. "My books."

"It's the air conditioner," he said. "It's outside. Looks like all the damage is out there, but we're checking. If it's contained, your books will be fine. Are you alone here? People? Pets?"

"Just me," she said. The fire was outside? She was probably less close to getting killed than he suggested, but admittedly she hadn't known that.

"Building clear," he said to his radio. Then he relieved her of the fire extinguisher, which, frankly she'd forgotten she held. "You're lucky you weren't hurt. And that no one was hurt looking for you."

"I'm *sorry*," she told him. "I had a clear view of the back and didn't see any flames."

"And then the goddamned ceiling collapses," he said, so fiercely she took a step back.

He sighed. "I'm sorry. I overreacted, but you underreacted. Next time, get out." He paused to listen to communication on his radio. "Better yet," he continued when the radio fell silent, "let's just skip the next time. You okay? Need another ambulance?"

He just had to throw that "another" in there, didn't he? She hugged herself, still shaky from the adrenaline. "This was *not* my fault," she said, wishing she hadn't given up the canister so easily. She tried to peer around him to see the fate of her store through the back door, but he was too tall. "And I didn't ride in the first one. What are you doing here anyway? I thought you had bridge duty."

He'd turned to look back inside, and when he met her eyes again he seemed to have relaxed a notch or ten, which went a long way toward convincing her everything really was okay. "Well," he said, one side of his mouth quirked, "I'm on shift, and if there's a fire, I tend to go to those. Even when they're in Wyoming."

God, must he know *everything*? "I panicked," she said, feeling her face heat. "You know, because of the fire."

He…chortled. Was that an actual thing? If not, he'd probably just made it one. "You're afraid of fire *and* water?"

Of course. Instead of saying something nice, like how *most* people tended to run in the opposite direction of fire, he had to be a jerk. She glared. "How many people do you know who *want* to burn to the ground?"

He grinned, and she hated herself for how attractive he was to her. Even covered in that white stuff from the fire extinguisher, some of the remnants of which he'd transferred to her when he'd hauled her out of the building.

"How many people who don't want to burn to the ground send the fire department to another state?" he asked.

She wished he'd vacate the steps. He stood between her and the building, and while keeping her away from the scene was almost certainly the point, she didn't need him towering over her. "Are you the only firefighter in this city? Or is there someone else who can berate me?"

"*Berate* you?" He laughed. "Need I remind you that just this morning you had two engines, an ambulance, two police cars, *and* a boat out here for you, and that half the town clapped when you stepped off the bridge? I think you're running a little loose and fast with the word *berate*." He glanced at the back of the bookstore. "Especially for a librarian."

"I am not a librarian," she said, irritated that he made it sound like a bad word, and equally so that she'd been prompted to spit out a denial. "I own this store, from which I intend to sell books. Maybe you should read one sometime… see what a real hero is like."

His eyes grew unexpectedly stormy, but the cloud left so quickly she wasn't sure she'd seen it. "Is that why you're afraid of everything? You can't deal with reality because life is supposed to be like the books?"

"I froze on the bridge," she said through clenched teeth. Anyone who had nearly lost their entire family in a flash flood would understand that, not that she owed him an explanation. "And most of us are a bit unpracticed in dealing with fire. Again, hardly everything." She conveniently ignored the fact that both had happened within a space of a few hours. That part didn't work in her favor. "You don't even know me, so stop trying to analyze me."

"What about skydiving? You afraid of that, too?" He'd ignored her request, still blocked her from her property, and now he was smirking. Her earlier instincts to kick him had been spot on, only now he stood six inches higher on the step, and with her below-average height she'd be lucky to bruise his ankle.

As for his skydiving question, it was hardly fair, considering the bridge. "How many times have *you* jumped out of a plane?"

He made some kind of *tsk* noise that did nothing to improve her opinion of him. "Twice. What about spiders?"

"How many people like spiders?" This was ridiculous. Her bookstore was on fire, and the fire department wanted to know if she liked spiders? She actually didn't care one way or another about bugs, whether they had eight legs or six, but why was she even talking to him? Her first instinct every time was to avoid confrontation. They were on solid ground. Walking away from him should have been easy, but she didn't want to give him the satisfaction.

His radio squawked a bunch of code talk, none of which Lieutenant Ego bothered to translate. "Is the store okay?"

He gave her a somber look. "With you at the helm? It's not looking good."

She planted her hands on her hips so she wouldn't be so tempted to punch him. "You are the biggest ass."

He adopted a serious countenance. "Your store is fine," he said, his voice all businesslike. "Your air conditioner took itself out of service. We'll make sure that's the extent of things before we leave. Do you have any fans?"

Her mind flew to the Facebook page she'd set up for the store before she left Wyoming. The one with six likes. "People who like me?"

He blinked, like she was the dumbest person on earth. "No," he said slowly. "The kind that move air. You've got a lot of smoke to clear out."

"Oh." She was losing count of the number of embarrassing moments a person could have in one day. "I'll get some." Her mind shifted to her bank account. Great. Fans probably cost a fortune.

"There's a hardware store right around the corner. I know the owner. He has a couple he keeps in the warehouse to move the air on hot days. I'll let him know what's going on up front, but I'm betting if you go talk to him he'll be happy to bring them down for you to use for a day or two."

Um, wow. "That's exceptionally kind of you," she said. "Thanks."

"I'd like to take the credit for being a nice guy," he said, "but in doing so I must also confess I'm trying to avoid getting a smoke inhalation call during dinner."

"Believe me, I don't want to see you again, either." She grumbled the words without forethought.

Much to his amusement, suggested by his grin.

Holy awkward hell. She had never been so embarrassed. Not. Ever. Her gaze dropped to her toes, but not without taking in the extinguisher-splattered view of Lt. Hottie. There had to be a casual way out of this situation. What did a person do to get rid of a fireman who had saved her twice in one day? She couldn't offer him a drink or anything…not with her place currently cordoned off, though if it was contained to the

AC unit, which had apparently been removed, she'd probably be back to work soon.

He cleared his throat, dragging her attention to his utterly handsome face. She'd love to see him with stubble, just a bit more rugged, but she'd read somewhere firefighters couldn't have facial hair. Was that a universal thing? And why was she standing there thinking how good he looked when she was a hot mess? She hated to think what she looked like. She hated even more that she thought to care. And she *really* hated how weak her knees felt. *Adrenaline*. Her life investment had almost burned down. She was definitely allowed a weak moment, as long as she didn't faint into his arms.

"I've never been sprayed with a fire extinguisher on my way into a building," he said, though this time his tone had softened. Not teasing her, then. She looked around. Where was the rest of his crew?

"Ms. Tyler?"

Lt. Hendricks knew her name. And he watched her. She lost a blip of a moment to the absolute intensity of those coffee-colored eyes. When she opened her mouth to speak, she managed only to close it without saying a word. Her heart hammered. She chalked it up to a delayed reaction to the fact that her store had almost burned down. Or, maybe smoke had just blown in. Either way, she was entitled to freak out a little.

His radio squawked yet another round of gibberish. He listened, then appeared to ignore it. "Why don't you head down to the hardware store? Unless we get another call, I'll be here to keep an eye on things, and when they bring the fans down I can help you set them up."

"I think I can plug in a fan." Damn her shaky voice. But it had been one of those days, and she'd had way too much caffeine.

His mouth tipped into a soft grin. "And I think I can help you with placement to maximize the speed at which they do their job."

"Okay." She felt like an idiot. Again. "Thank you," she sputtered at the last minute, trying not to sound ungrateful. What was it about this town that flustered her? As if she didn't know.

As if those melty-chocolate eyes weren't watching her that very moment.

She blinked, using the excuse to break eye contact. "I'm going to need my handbag out of the store."

"Where is it?"

"On the table in the back room."

"Wait here." He disappeared, moving easily despite the bulk of his gear, and returned a moment later with her bag. She accepted it, but he didn't release his grip when she began to turn away.

Startled, she met his eyes.

"You know," he said. "You ran toward the fire."

She blinked, unsure what to do with his statement of the obvious. "With a fire extinguisher."

That now-familiar grin touched his lips and made her ache inside. He probably had that effect on a lot of women, though the thought didn't tamp down her own appreciation of his smile.

"So," he said, "maybe you're not as afraid of everything as you thought you were."

"Maybe," she said. But she left the rest unspoken. Because it was much more likely she wasn't afraid enough.

Especially when it came to him. Anyone who could disarm a hyperventilating woman off a bridge the way he had absolutely deserved wariness.

"I think you need to face your fears," he said, in such a serious tone that she fully expected him to come back with news of a fear-facing class or support group, probably held right across the bridge.

Her eyes narrowed. "I'm pretty sure you said I just did."

He shook his head. "No, more than that. Get out and have some fun. I bet you'd love whitewater rafting."

Had she told him she didn't have fun? So maybe bridges were a stretch and she had some trouble buttoning her blouse. That didn't mean she was a loser who needed to *get out*. Especially not whitewater rafting. Been there, done that, albeit in a pickup, but that night wasn't the kind of thing a person just shook off. "*No*."

He glanced toward the mountains that gave the town its western edge. "What about a hike to a waterfall?"

Now he was just mocking her. How professional. She should have his badge, or shield, or whatever fire officers were awarded, revoked. "Torrents of rushing water?" she asked, incredulous. "You think that sounds like something I'd enjoy?"

"What if it's just a trickle?"

She crossed her arms and hoped her glare would reach him, the way he towered over her. Was that why he stood on that step? A power play? "I've yet to run from a running faucet, if that's what you mean. And I don't appreciate being the butt of your jokes. If you're going to mock me, do it behind my back."

The smirk left his mouth. "I'm not mocking you," he told her with a surprising amount of sincerity. "But if you don't get past at least one of your fears, you're going to become a drain on city resources."

She rolled her eyes and hoped it hid her cringe, because she knew he was right, and she'd have been fine to hear it from anyone but him. The man pushed all her buttons. "How very gallant of you. If it makes you feel better, I won't call on you for help again."

He tilted his head. "*Or*, how about instead of letting the store burn to the ground or stopping cross-town traffic, you just face your fears?"

"I *tried*. Which is how I ended up frozen on the bridge in the first place." And if the success of that attempt was any indication, the best way for her to keep her hands out of the city resource coffers was to steer clear of fear-facing situations.

"That was admirable, I guess, but how about you take a slightly smaller first step?"

"What, with you?" As soon as the words left her mouth, she realized there hadn't been any *we* in his suggestion. None whatsoever.

He blinked. "Yeah," he said slowly. "With me. Someone has to keep this town safe from you. Ideally someone trained to deal with emergencies."

Her heart flipped and tumbled around a big, flashing, neon sign screaming *bad idea*. Way past time to backpedal. "It would hardly be fair of me to rob this town of its savior," she told him. "Maybe you have a friend who could go with me instead?" One last-ditch effort to get rid of *this* guy.

"Not a chance," he said.

She tried to force a smile. "I'm sure there's someone less…busy." Never mind that she seemed to be the source of his tight schedule.

"Nice try," he said. "But if anyone is going to send you down the river on a raft, it's going to be me."

Chapter Four

Twenty-four hour shifts with the Dry Rock FD didn't leave Shane fatigued. They left him restless. He normally capped off those hours of being on call with a strenuous hike through the mountains that jackknifed the western sky, but today he found himself standing in front of Shelf Indulgence. A bookstore, of all places. He had absolutely nothing against reading—especially not good old-fashioned paper books— but there weren't any mountains to climb within those walls, which thankfully stood unscathed. They'd removed the smoke-spewing window-unit air conditioner, and the brick exterior wall bore only the faintest scar.

The door didn't have a sign indicating whether the place was open or what the hours might be. He hadn't shut down the building, but she'd only arrived in town yesterday. Hardly enough time to get the paperwork in order, especially after the way her day had gone.

For that matter, he wasn't sure if she'd made it back across the bridge, let alone twice. He should have looked up her address—one not in Wyoming—but what would be the point? He'd be gone in two weeks. He'd gotten her off the bridge and they'd kept her building from burning down. His job was done.

So why, instead of tearing up those mountains, was he knocking on her bookstore door?

And why the hell did he forget his name when she opened it?

If she'd been gorgeous the day before, today she took his breath and stomped on his chest. And that was before she smiled. She didn't look different, exactly, so he wasn't sure why she left him reeling. Maybe it was the openness of her expression. Maybe it was the way her eyes lit when she saw him. At least that's what he wanted to think, or else his visceral reaction was seriously overkill.

"Hey," she said, like they were old friends.

Bewildered, he glanced over his shoulder. Nope. No one there but him. "Uh, hey."

"I'm glad you're here. Come in."

He stepped inside, though now as suspicious of her intentions as he was of his own. She wore the same clothes as the day before, he finally realized, though she'd managed to correctly button her shirt. Still, had she spent the night at the store? Only one way to find out. "I guess you made it across the bridge this morning?"

She hesitated. "Actually, no. I stayed here. But if that's some sort of code violation, yes, I made it home and back just fine. And I wanted to thank you," she rushed on, not giving him a chance to comment on her sleeping arrangement, "for yesterday."

"You're welcome?" Was this a sane version of this woman? Maybe this was what happened when one didn't begin the day terrified on a bridge and round it out with a small fire. It should have been a good thing, but instead of relishing her apparent lack of fight, he found he missed it.

Very few women batted more than their eyelashes at him, and this one had thrown nothing but roadblocks.

Her eyes hitched to his at his questioning tone. "No, I mean it," she said. "You're clearly good at your job. I thought you were being unprofessional, but you read me…well, like a book. So thank you, and, um, of course I won't hold you to having to see me again. The justice system forgives statements made under duress, so I can do the same."

He stared while her words tumbled over one another in their rush to get out. She didn't want to see him again? He should have been thrilled. The woman was afraid to cross bridges, for heaven's sake, and he rushed toward danger at every turn. Plus, he was moving in two weeks. He couldn't begin to guess what else they didn't have in common, but it didn't matter. He was as good as gone.

He watched as she fought to hold her smile, then realized his suspicions had been on point. She really didn't want him there.

He'd rescued her twice in one day, and she had to *fake* a smile?

"You're probably right," he said, only pretending to agree with her. "If you can't handle that bridge, there's no way you can handle me. Much better you stay somewhere safe. In fact, I could use the peace and quiet of a bookstore." He vaguely remembered a sofa from his quick trip through the day before, and he found it in a corner before she had a chance to object. A faint smoke smell lingered, but she had the windows open and the fans on. Fresh mountain air poured in, only a hint of the city on its heels. He flopped onto the cushions, which gave more than he expected, but if she'd noticed the unceremonious landing, she didn't flinch.

She bit her lip, leaving him with an ungodly urge to follow her bite with one of his own. "I'm not…open," she said.

He ignored her and his stupidly clawing urge to kiss her.

"Do I smell coffee?"

"It's cinnamon roll."

He inhaled, sure he smelled otherwise. "Not coffee?"

"No, it's coffee, but cinnamon roll flavored."

He blinked. "How is that coffee?" Coffee was supposed to be black and rich. Not...fluffy.

She pasted on a gratuitous smile. "Perhaps you should go to a convenience store for something more your speed."

"I happen to enjoy a good cinnamon roll," he said. He had no desire to drink one, but he didn't throw that in. Plus, she hadn't mentioned Starbucks, which he considered a huge plus. "I'd love some."

She crossed her arms, though it was the only falter in her facade of friendly professionalism. "I didn't offer."

He glanced around the space. It was cluttered and a bit unkempt. That was to be expected, but it still reminded him of his grandma's living room. "Can you recommend any reading material to go with my cinnamon-roll coffee?" Ignoring her was getting tough. He wanted to call her out, get her all riled up, and wait for the hurricane to blow through, but she remained steadfast. To a fault.

"I'm still getting organized," she said primly.

He held his arms out wide, accidentally whacking the windowsill with one hand and nudging a cardboard box nearly off the end table with another. He righted the box then returned her saccharine smile with one of his own. "And yet I see books."

"Fine." She smiled, and it was so tight he was surprised by the effort, but she spun on her toe and walked away.

He settled against the cushions and checked out the store, this time without the benefit of smoke and a fire crew at his back. The space wasn't large, and with five short lengths of stacks dominating the room, the impression of his grandma's place gave way to that of an elementary school library. A couple of long paper bookmarks poked from the lines of volumes on the shelves. He wondered if she'd begun inventory, or if that was where the last owners had left off. The proprietors before her had been an elderly couple, and the few times he'd stopped by he'd noticed their tastes tended toward the eccentric, but his last visit had been years ago. The place had closed down for a couple of years without any interest from a buyer.

Then Caitlin showed up out of the blue, or fresh from Wyoming, as it turned out. He found himself wondering what her plans were.

And then, why he cared.

She returned in short order with a coffee mug, handing it to him without a word before leaving again.

He read the cup. *I'm single, because apparently the only good men are fictional.* He grinned. This woman clearly had no idea how much he loved a challenge.

The *squeak* of a metal cart with poorly greased wheels caught his attention. "Reading material," she said, handing him a book off the top. "I haven't had time to get through much, but I'm sure these will do."

He glanced at the book title. *History of Childbirth.* Fully illustrated, with a knobby brown exterior and crispy yellowed pages that looked and smelled to be a hundred years old. "It's been a few months since my last paramedic recertification," he said. "This might be useful."

Her polite, albeit strained, smile faltered, but she pulled it together with a subtly deep breath that not-so-subtly pushed her breasts against her blouse, straining the buttons. "If there's anything else you need…"

She let the words trail off, like she couldn't bear to finish the offer, and he had to bury his nose in the musty book to hide his grin.

There was something else he needed all right.

And when she realized what he had in mind, Caitlin Tyler wouldn't know what hit her.

• • •

Caitlin was going to kill Lt. Shane Hendricks. It had been four hours. Four hours of him pleasantly turning pages through musty old medieval childbirth manuals and feminist essays. They should have been the least of all topics interesting to a Neanderthal who thought he was God's gift, but a few stolen peeks through the stacks assured her he was, in fact, reading. Either that or taking the joke too far, but the steady shift of his eyes across the page indicated otherwise. Irritation waged war against pride. He *wanted* her to throw him out.

Which meant she had to tolerate his existence.

If only that was all she did.

She tried, hard, to focus on inventory, but—worst pun ever not intended—the man was on *fire*. He'd been hot enough in his bulky work jacket, which was beyond not fair. If she wore something that thick and drab, she'd look like she was caught in a burlap sack. But on him, it was rugged.

Without it, no less so.

She feared the lack of clothing between them. Whatever fire retardant gear he'd worn the day before had been a sufficient barrier—one suggestive enough of that God's gift hero complex thing he had going on. The one that left him smirking at her while she almost died on a bridge. And again in a fire.

The one that made her want to keep her distance.

Today, though, she wanted to climb onto his lap and slide down the fire pole. She didn't know if the firehouse had one, but she knew the fire guy did.

Damn him.

It had been too long since she'd had sex. The last time had

been a rebound thing with a guy who volunteered shelving books at the library. It was so cute it was almost book-worthy, but sixty seconds of frantic-on-his-part missionary on a well-worn carpet in the reference section hadn't been hot. No orgasm to show for the rug burn. Not cool. And then the guy wouldn't quit calling.

Guys like Shane, on the other hand, rarely bothered to call at all.

So maybe he had a thing going for him.

A thing other than sinful hotness.

She must have sighed, because at that moment her heart did the swoony thing, he glanced up and somehow managed to meet her eyes through the narrow view she had of him between volumes lined on the metal shelves. She blinked and jerked away, only to realize she'd just arranged a half dozen gardening books in a section on international politics.

"Private Sex Advice to Women," he said, making her jump.

This was ridiculous. It was her store. Maybe it hadn't burned down because of him, or at least the rest of his shift had handled it while he goaded her, but that didn't give him an unlimited open-door policy.

"I'm not interested in your advice," she muttered.

"It's a book," he said. "So far you've given me childbirth, feminism, and sex. Is there a message here?"

Yes, yes there was. A message not to hang out in her store.

"An ABZ of Love." The sound of flipping pages cracked the silence. "Hey, did you know alcohol can provide a form of substitute for a reasonably harmonious sex life?"

"You're not getting me drunk," she said, though she made a note to research if that might be true. As if a bottle of anything could compare to the smallest touch from a guy like him.

"I don't recall offering," he told her. His tone could have

been teasing, though she didn't know him well enough to make that call. All she knew was that her face was on fire, and it would just have to burn because there was no way she was putting in another call to the fire department, even if he clearly wasn't on duty at the moment. "But," he added, "if it's a substitute for sex, and you're refusing it, does that mean you've found other forms of self-plea—"

"*Stop*. Enough." God, she hoped he was only there until she gave in, because otherwise she was about to make a huge fool of herself. Again. "I'll do one thing. *One*. One non-sexual, non-alcoholic thing on what is absolutely *not* going to be a date, and then we're done."

She'd managed to emerge from the stacks before spitting out the entire sentence, which meant she had an unobstructed view of his infuriatingly cocky grin when he closed the book.

"I thought you'd never ask."

Chapter Five

If Shane felt the tiniest bit guilty for low-key stalking to get his definitely-not-a-date with Caitlin, that feeling vanished the next night when he saw her. And it shouldn't have, at least not in the conventional sense. She wasn't dressed to kill, so to speak, but she slayed him anyway. She'd traded her proper skirt and button-up shirt for a pair of tight polka-dot leggings that hugged every curve, all phenomenally on display when the breeze hit her just right, but modesty reigned with an oversize shirt that offered no hint of the cleavage he'd noticed through her misbuttoned blouse. A pair of ankle boots evened the odds by a few inches, but the clunky heels were more cute than sexy.

Especially with her hair up and slender neck begging for the heat of his mouth.

She hadn't given him her address, and he hadn't reminded her how easily he could obtain it on his own. Instead, she'd agreed to meet him, and he'd made sure he was there first. Convenient, because he might have slipped into horny teenager territory when she walked up, splayed tips of her hair bouncing away from that messy bun, as carefree as he'd ever seen anyone.

Let alone someone he'd met clinging to a bridge.

He'd gotten a kick out of riling her earlier, but now it was *him* feeling off-balance, while she stunned. And he definitely needed the benefit of the table blocking his lap from her view. Despite which, he stood to greet her.

A couple of guys called his name. He replied with an absent wave of his hand, not taking his eyes off her.

"You showed," he said when she stopped in front of him.

Her eyes glittered with amusement. Or maybe resignation. "It's not like you were going to let me off the hook if I didn't. This is happening under false pretenses."

His lips quirked. "Why is that?"

"I don't date."

He wondered what she left unspoken. The why. The reason he'd become an exception. Not that it mattered, though. He was moving to Denver in two weeks. More like twelve days now, not that he counted. "I'm not looking for someone to date, so I say that makes me the perfect person to show you around."

"Is that what you're doing? Because I'm remarkably capable of reading a map."

"Until there's a bridge to cross."

She flushed and threw him an adorably dirty look. At which point he realized she must have actually crossed the bridge, unless she bought new clothes and conjured that freshly-showered, soapy smell out of thin air. "I do have to thank you for that," she said. "Although it can't be good for your ego to know the lengths to which a woman will go to get away from you."

"And yet here you are."

"And for what purpose? Are you going to teach me to stop, drop, and roll?"

"There are laws against teaching those lessons in public," he said, taking advantage of her surprise by touching her arm, guiding her away from the square toward the park wedged between the city and the mountains. It seemed mostly a way to make use of the craggy, undevelopable land at the city's edge, though it had turned into one of the most frequented hotspots. This section was narrow, with just a feeder trail that wove along the downtown district, providing a bit of green reprieve that was especially popular midday. "But if you want to go somewhere private, I'd be glad to help you with your moves."

She blinked. "Tell me that line doesn't work. Please tell me it has *never* worked."

"You say that like I *need* lines." Yeah, so he'd made that sound bad, but there was a degree of truth there. Which had to be why he liked her so much.

Her steps slowed as they neared a trailhead. "I'm not going in there."

He gave her credit for street smarts, assuming that was the reason behind her refusal. Heading into the loosely-knit woods with a near-stranger definitely deserved second thought, but he didn't hear dubious regret. He heard fear. "Why not?"

"Because you just offered to take me somewhere private, and now you're trying to lead me into the woods." She threw the excuse out like a jab, but he detected a hint of worry behind it.

"I'm not taking you in the woods to roll around in the dirt." He paused. "At least not until you ask."

"Yeah, that'll happen. But seriously, I *actually* cannot go in there."

He looked from her to the seemingly innocuous trail and back. Maybe she was less worried about him than he thought. "I don't smell smoke, and we're on solid ground, and it's not even humid, so water can't be the problem. Why can't you go?"

She worried her lip, and that confidence—or was it just bravado?—slipped a notch. "It's dark in there."

He blinked. Though it wasn't late, the sun had already dipped behind the mountaintops, leaving the sky streaked with color. The woods were shadowy, maybe, but not anything close to blackout conditions. "Dark?"

She raised her shoulders, straightening her spine. "Yes."

He studied her, realizing how thin that bravado actually was. "You're afraid of the dark?"

"Maybe." Her voice wavered, but her chin jutted in defiance.

He sighed. So they were going to do this thing again, where she got annoyed with him to hide her own fears.

In just a couple of cumulative hours of acquaintance, they had that routine down. But this time he saw the vulnerability behind the front. Pushing her dinged at his conscience, but he also knew it got results.

"Walk with me," he said, hoping his sincerity got through to her. "It's a *walk*. And I promise not to leave you alone out there."

He saw the wheels turning. And the sinking sun reflected in the greenest eyes he'd ever seen, making him want more than anything for her to agree. "No bridges?" she finally asked.

He ignored that question, and for good reason. Instead, he said, "Isn't the dark the best time to cross a bridge?"

For someone who was afraid of pretty much everything, she sure managed to skewer him with a look.

"Fine," he said. "I brought you here because there's a bridge. But it's not that big. You have my word I won't make you cross it if you don't want to."

"You want me to cross a bridge in the dark?" He couldn't

tell if she was more skeptical or worried. Frankly, he didn't blame her for either. Or himself for being intrigued. He worked with men who ran toward danger, and this woman not only avoided it, she'd invented it.

He should be going in the absolute opposite direction.

Instead, he said, "There's a creek and a sunset. If we start walking now, that is."

He was absolutely convinced she was going to walk, straight back out of the park, but instead she met his eyes and hit him with an utterly charming smile.

One that scared the hell out of him.

"Okay," she finally said. "You're on."

• • •

Caitlin had long realized she had a few quirks, but having to lay them all out in quick succession to the hot fire guy made them feel more ridiculous than they ever had before. She could probably explain that she'd been with her family when their truck was swept away by a flash flood, that boiling, churning water would never be okay, and that she'd probably never see a black sky and not remember that horrible night, but that'd be revealing more than she ever shared. With anyone.

She wanted to be more irritated with Shane than she was. He'd coerced her into meeting him, and then chose something he knew terrified her. Hell, the whole town probably knew about her and bridges by now. Between her determination to lay low and the fact that her store wasn't yet open, she'd at least managed to avoid having it thrown in her face. Mostly.

The Uber driver who'd shuttled her across the bridge that morning had mentioned an incident, eyebrows raised as he glanced in the rearview mirror, but she just smiled and nodded her agreement that it was, indeed, a good thing traffic was moving that day.

Shane had been there, though. He'd seen her panic.

And his idea of a gathering spot had been a bridge.

She sighed, inadvertently drawing his attention, obliterating her determination to stay brutal. She hated her fears, and hated even more that she'd wound up revealing them to hero guy. He ran into burning buildings. She hyperventilated when her air conditioner smoked.

"I love these mountains when the sun sets," he said, and she realized he'd left her to her inner turmoil, forcing her to grudgingly respect that he hadn't thrown her failings back out there. But unlike every other woman he professed to knowing, she didn't swoon when he opened his mouth. Maybe he'd finally figured that out.

Despite a suspicion that he was dropping yet another cliché on her—sunsets and walks on the beach were the ones to end them all—she followed his gaze, and her breath caught at the colors skimming the mountaintops. "Wow," she murmured.

"It never gets old," he said. "There's not a day it doesn't take my breath."

She'd always loved sunsets but didn't think that was much of a guy thing. "Are you from here?"

"Nope. Denver. My mom moved the family here after my dad died, but I can't say it ever felt like home. The mountains remind me of there, though."

"I'm sorry about your father," she said.

"I think of him when the sun turns the snow up there orange and yellow."

She wasn't sure what to say, and he didn't seem to expect a response. They settled into an amicable silence. The trail wound through relatively flat, relatively sparse woods, and she was grateful for the turns that made walking side-by-side a less obvious proposition. Though the alternatives kind of sucked. There was no way she'd walk ahead of him, where he might possibly sneak up on her from behind, which left her watching him.

Muscle shouldn't look so good beneath a loose-fitting T-shirt.

The man probably didn't have an ounce of fat on his body, but he wasn't some overly bulked up gym worshiper. He definitely worked out but didn't have those stupid squared off muscles that couldn't get out of their own way. Nope, he was long and lean and perfect for sliding between sheets.

Which was where her mind was when she walked into his back.

"Sorry," she said, righting her glasses rather than looking at him. Then she heard the rush of water and glanced past him to see a terrifying expanse of footbridge, and she gawked. Directly at him, probably looking stupid as hell. "*This* is a nothing bridge?"

It wasn't crazy high, and the water beneath it didn't rage, but it definitely flowed several feet below. She couldn't fathom why he thought this a good idea, but she had two guesses: mockery, or torture. And she'd believe either.

But he didn't look all proud of himself, like he'd set her up. "You've made it across worse," he said. "Besides, I can tell you in official capacity that you can't live in the bookstore, because it's against code, and this is one fear you're definitely going to need to get past if you're going to live here. So, you're welcome. Now come on."

She stared in absolute disbelief. "This is you doing me a favor?"

"Yes, minus the sirens and the guys in the ambulance and the fact we had to drag out the boat." His humor softened, and she almost expected him to say something sweet. Instead, he said, "You afraid?"

She glared at him. "*Yes*, I'm afraid."

"Good. Face it. Head on."

"I *am* facing it. And now I'd like to face the other direction."

"Fine. Close your eyes."

"What?"

"Close your eyes."

She stared at him a long time before finally doing as he asked. Immediately after which she was hoisted off the ground and carried. Somewhere. She didn't dare look, though the *clomp* of his feet across wood suggested the damned bridge. *On the bridge and in his arms.* There wasn't anything romantic about the way he lifted her, but she still felt all tingly and a lot less concerned with her predicament than she should have been.

He set her down. Not on firm ground, she noticed when she dared to look at her feet, but on the bridge. The gaps between the planks were enough to see water. The warm-and-fuzzies fled.

She bit back a scream, but then thought twice about it. Why not scream? Someone would find her. Perhaps someone a little less sadistic, though at this point she wasn't sure which was worse—that he'd taken her to yet another bridge, or that her thoughts were still stuck on the way his touch made her feel.

"Look at me," he said.

She did, and ten pounds of tension left her shoulders when his melted-chocolate gaze touched hers.

"You've done this before, and over much worse," he said. "I've got you."

What if she was more worried about him than the bridge? What then? She didn't ask. Instead, she said, "You promised you wouldn't make me." Weak defense, but she had to throw something out there. No way she would let these electrical squiggles in her chest go unchecked.

"And I still won't," he said, yet he made no move to rescue

her. "There's no depth to that water. Depending on the rocks, maybe knee deep at most. You're not going to drown."

"I thought you could drown in a teaspoon of water."

He smiled, and she immediately thought of a toothpaste commercial. "Hey," he said. "I'm FD. No way I'd risk my reputation over a teaspoon of water."

"That's comforting," she grumbled. Sarcasm touched her thoughts, but she couldn't deny the truth of the words. If landing ankle deep in a creek meant he'd put his arms around her, she'd probably be willing to risk it.

"The rails are solid," he said in that same even, steady tone. "So is the bridge. The whole thing was just replaced two years ago. If you want to look, the wood is still bright, not weathered gray."

Some kid jumped on the edge of the bridge behind Shane, and the whole thing shook. "Lovely. I'll leave a glowing review for park maintenance."

"I'm sure they'll appreciate that. Now walk."

"Toward you?" It should have been an easy task, but the visceral reaction she'd had to the cross-town bridge lingered, and her chest grew tighter by the second. Sputtering through a tight breath, she said, "I'm pretty sure that's the opposite of what worked last time."

"Want me to squeeze behind you?"

Um, no, no she did not. "There will be no squeezing on this bridge." As she spoke, another kid ran past them, jostling her toward the edge. It wasn't much of a risk on paper, the railings being what they were, but taking that side step terrified her. And for some reason, she looked down. "Oh God."

"Hey." Shane touched her palm. Not exactly holding her hand, but definitely grabbing her attention, where it lingered, as did he. Instinctively, she curled her fingertips around his. She'd have to live that down later. Right now, she really didn't want to die on that stupid footbridge. She fought panic, praying for breath to touch her lungs. She hated how childish she felt, but even without the whole story, he of all people should understand. In some capacity, it was his *job* to understand.

"Look at me," he said, "then put one foot in front of the other."

"If I don't look down, am I really facing my fears?" A weak joke. Any chance to argue and not acknowledge all the tingly feelings that spread warmth from her fingertips to her belly. Her head buzzed, and at this point she didn't know whether to blame her fear or the man intent on stoking it.

"Just walk," he told her, a smile playing at his lips. He tugged at her hand, walking backward, holding her hostage with those alluring brown eyes that had morphed in low light from warm chocolate to rich espresso. Was there such a thing as chocolate espresso? If not, someone really needed to get right on that.

She winced as her foot bobbled on a fallen stick. Eyes pegged on his chest, which was the safest possible direction, she muttered, "If I survive this, I will find you."

"Sweetheart, I'm counting on it."

She gave him a sharp look, only to find him grinning. Some rebellious inner part of her turned to mush. He really was handsome. As much as she hated the whole player stereotype and the implication that she somehow wasn't worthy, she had to admit to herself that having his attention on her was flattering. Her, with her glasses sliding down her nose and her thighs quaking over a stupid bridge…yeah, that was exactly why her thighs quaked.

He tugged her, gently enough, but still pulling her off-balance. She thumped against his chest, panic welling in the split second it took her to imagine they'd hit the rail together and go sprawling to their deaths, but he didn't budge. Instead of flailing, she took a deep breath of something woodsy and soapy. God, he smelled good.

And this was so, so bad.

Anyone passing by might have thought they were having a moment, her head against his chest, their fingers wound tight. She kneed him in the thigh.

"Hey!" He jerked back, like he thought he was protecting himself, when the truth was she was too short to easily hit the bullseye and too nice to make hard contact. But let him think what he wanted. He'd put her on this stupid bridge.

She poked him in the chest, any relief at not feeling alone spewing forth as defense. "What makes you think I need rescuing?"

He blinked. "I'm guessing it's the *actual fact* that you needed rescuing twice this week already."

"And this?" She gestured underfoot, before she could dwell on what had been an excellent point. "*This* is supposed to help me get across five lanes of vibrating concrete?"

Okay, so she was irrationally annoyed, but that beat the hell out of breaking down and crying. She'd never felt so stupid in her life.

It was *just a bridge*.

She swallowed a hiccup-sob before it escaped, almost choking on it. Not even a deep breath of evergreen-scented air was enough to calm the panic welling in her chest.

"Would you rather I show up every morning and walk you across?" His tone had lost some of the tease, and for a moment she wondered if he might be serious. Like being reminded of her failings every single day would be a good thing.

"Why would you offer to walk me across?" she asked. "Wouldn't driving someone who's terrified make more sense?"

He tilted his head. "Are you asking me for a ride?"

"No."

"Because I give great rides."

The heat of a thousand suns touched her face. Her mind dove straight into the gutter, conjuring up an image that probably wasn't the kind of ride he had in mind. Or maybe it was exactly what he had in mind. She wasn't sure which was worse. Either way, not happening. She had to live in Dry Rock. Getting her heart broken by a man who had already told her he wasn't interested, yet still managed to spend every waking moment in her face, wasn't going to make for a pleasant fresh start.

She swallowed, audibly and awkwardly. "Is that what this city asks of its public servants? Training exercises with its most pathetic citizens?"

A breeze touched her skin, lifting a lock of hair that had escaped from its knot. He pushed it back with his free hand, letting his fingertips linger.

She was standing on a bridge, water rushing underfoot, and the only thing she felt were butterflies.

Score one for the Lieutenant.

"Just so we're clear," he said gently, "I'm off the clock. You're not a work project."

Totally benign words, but spoken low they made her heart race. It didn't matter that he hadn't denied the rest of what she'd said. He'd told her he was there of his own accord, and that made those butterflies wiggle like crazy in her chest. She suspected he could whisper the ingredients off a box of macaroni and cheese and make her want to drag him into bed.

"And now I'm on the bridge," she managed to say, but damn every shaky word. If she'd been on solid ground with a reasonable expectation of staying there, she would have loved how green the space was. Her world in Wyoming had been an endless sea of drab prairie grasses. This was nothing short of lush by comparison, and the flowers that seemed to burst from every available sunlit groove only cemented that point.

He touched her hip, at which point she realized he still held her now sweaty hand. "Good."

She needed a moment to remember what she'd said. Bragging about standing on the same bridge two kids had no problem racing across. *Show-offs*. "Um, I'd like to not be on the bridge any longer."

"Do I need to rescue you?" Humor danced in his words, but there was a solidarity there. Maybe it was her lust-driven ovaries doing the talking, but she kind of believed he was on her side.

Which was, in all likelihood, a huge mistake. "Or," she said, "move out of my way. Because, as I recall, you are off the clock."

He obliged, but by stepping to the side, forcing *her* to step close to the side to get around him. Which she did, not because she wasn't afraid, but because she didn't want to give him the satisfaction of her refusal.

So what if she saw stars and heard a dull roar from the universe? She made it. She could just hyperventilate quietly, maybe keep the paramedics uninvolved, maybe never look at another bridge again.

He gave her a moment, which she sort of appreciated and otherwise wished he'd do something to tick her off so she could focus on that instead. Annoying as he was, he wasn't bad to look at. Letting him distract her had to be better than being consumed by the threat of plunging to her death.

"Look up," he said, right behind her when he spoke.

She hadn't heard him approach over the sounds of fear and agony running laps inside her head. She turned to see him, but he wasn't looking at her, so she followed his gaze up. Through a break in the trees, the sky had deepened to a brilliant red that made the snow-topped mountains glow like lit matches. "Wow."

"Yeah."

She glanced his way to agree, but he was looking at her now. And there went the butterflies all over again. God, if ever there was a moment to be kissed, it was now, in the soft, muted world brought on by evening and sunset. *Score one for the clichés.* Not that she wanted him to kiss her. Kissing him would be a disaster. She'd think about it forever.

That didn't stop her from swaying toward him.

"Caitlin Tyler," he said in that low voice that made every word a seduction.

"Mmm— Yes?" Her voice bobbled. Oh God. This was it. He was going to kiss her. And she was *so* going there, because if there was ever a good time for a bad idea, it was now, with a guy like him.

"You are the most frustrating woman I've ever met."

His words jerked her out of her daze. Maybe she'd gotten carried away, but for him to tell her she annoyed him? Under *that* sunset?

There was only one thing she could say to that.

"Good."

Chapter Six

If Shane wanted to introduce Caitlin to the heartbeat of Dry Rock, there was no better place than his favorite diner. But now he second-guessed that decision. The number of patrons crammed in the joint pointed to the fact it was *everyone's* favorite. Hell, they were probably over capacity. He could just imagine the scene when the chief showed up and threw them all out for breaking the fire code. Caitlin would love that.

"Maybe we should have headed somewhere a bit less crowded," he said, after the tenth meet-and-greet in as many steps. "I didn't realize how often I stopped to talk to people until now. Everyone knows everyone around here."

"You say that like it's a bad thing. I worried about moving to a big city," she said wistfully. "I thought I'd miss knowing all of my neighbors, but you've given me hope for that feeling of community."

"You're slipping," he told her. "That almost sounded sincere." He couldn't imagine anyone considering this a big city, but he hadn't ridden in from the plains of Wyoming.

She smiled, and the warmth of the simple gesture made

him want to be somewhere else, all right. Somewhere private. But he'd fumbled that already back in the woods. He'd wanted to kiss her, thought he was going to do it—then he'd thought better of it and spit out the dumbest possible thing he could have said.

It had worked, at least. The appreciation on her face as the sun disappeared behind the jagged horizon had put a knot in his chest. A knot he couldn't afford. The schmuckiness had lingered after he'd shut things down, but fortunately so had the awkwardness of what he'd blurted out. At least he didn't have to worry about kissing her at the diner, not with half the town casting curious glances their way.

She shifted closer to avoid upending a tray of drinks, and his synapses misfired. If she turned to face him, she'd be indecently close. The thought made him want to spin her around. Embrace indecent. Instead, he diverted his attention to the back of the room, where his friends occupied their usual table. Somewhat relieved, he steered her in that direction. It was their only hope of being able to sit, but also finding it a great time to introduce her to a few people who, unlike him, planned on sticking around.

"I *am* sincere," she said, dragging his thoughts out of dangerous territory. "But that still doesn't mean I'm going to worship you."

The tail end of her proclamation hit the air just as they walked up on the table, leaving all four of its occupants staring at them in varying amounts of interest and amusement. "Guys," Shane said, his words rumbling his chest against her back. "You remember Ms. Tyler."

Caitlin not-so-subtly elbowed him in the stomach. "Caitlin," she said.

Shane slid into the three-quarter circle booth and gestured for Caitlin to follow. The group bunched to make room while he doled out introductions. "Matt, Diego, Jack,

Lexi. Everyone but Lex is on shift with me."

Matt's grin suggested Shane was going to have to punch him later. "So, in other words," Matt said to Caitlin, "we've met. Nice to see you without the sirens."

Lexi shot Matt a sideways look, but he didn't immediately elaborate, and Caitlin had already turned a solid shade of pink. Either Lexi noticed or defaulted to her habit of ignoring Matt, because she turned her attention to Caitlin, offering her a sympathetic smile. "It's great to meet you, Caitlin. And you have no idea how much I mean that, because being the only woman in this group of guys is only good when I set the kitchen on fire, trying to fix dinner, and only then because they put it out. Being reminded of it for months after the fact pretty much negates the benefits."

Caitlin's eyes widened. "You set fire to your kitchen?"

Shane hoped he kept his amusement from showing. Lexi had probably just found a friend for life with that confession. Though he wasn't sure the two of them belonged in a room together. Maybe they'd survive it if Caitlin manned the fire extinguisher when Lexi gave in to the inclination to cook.

Before Lexi could respond, Matt gave her a sidelong look. "How do you negate the benefits of *not* having your house burn down?"

Lexi rolled her eyes. "Hey, I didn't see *you* there throwing buckets of water."

Matt smirked. "That's because we have hoses for that kind of work."

Diego leaned back against the bright-red vinyl booth cushion, steepling his fingers across his abdomen. "Yeah, we're all packing enormous hoses."

Jack gave Caitlin a crooked smile and tipped his head toward Matt. "Well, when the fire happened, Matt here was at home in bed with his hose."

Shane would have given anything for a picture of Caitlin's

expression in that moment. It teetered between amusement and alarm, though there was no mistaking the way she'd relaxed next to him, her body softening rather than stiffening when his arm brushed hers. He could see her there with them, long-term. Without him. Which had been precisely his hope when he'd brought her over, but he hadn't expected the stab of emptiness that accompanied it.

Matt had turned his own shade of red, as he did every time Lexi's house fire was brought up. Shane figured it killed Matt not to have been among the Calvary swooping in to save Lex, but his friend had never come close to admitting that. "I was at home with the *flu*," he said. "And unlike yours," he added, giving Lexi a pointed look, "my hose doesn't detach. Where else would it be?"

Shane blinked. *This* was a new accusation. "You have a detachable hose?" he asked Lexi.

She blushed, diverting her attention to the chrome-edged table top, which was scattered with four nearly empty baskets of food and a matching number of cups. In the background, decades-old music played from what looked like a working jukebox. "It was a gag gift."

Across the table, Diego lost the battle to choke back laughter. "*Gag* gift."

"I still don't think Matt had the flu," Jack said. "He'd probably eaten her cooking."

"I can cook," Lexi said, a stubborn set to her jaw.

"The *dog* won't even eat your cooking," Matt said.

Despite the limited span of Shane's interactions with Caitlin, he had growing sympathy for Matt. Lexi was giving him the same look Caitlin had worn in almost all of their previous conversations, though Shane understood that her time thus far in Dry Rock had been…stressful. But tonight… tonight, something had begun to change between him and Caitlin.

Just not the fact that he was leaving, which meant nothing should change at all. At least not beyond her getting past a couple of her fears, because the thought of Jack or Diego swaggering in to save her made Shane want to preemptively put both men on the ground.

Caitlin, who had been watching Matt and Lexi go back and forth like they were on the courts of Wimbledon, asked, "Are you guys…dating?"

Shane understood her confusion. They acted more like an old married couple than anyone he knew, including old married couples.

"No," they responded in unison. "Neighbors," Lexi added.

"They share a dog," Shane said. The so-called explanation had persisted for years, and no one bought it. He wasn't even sure Matt or Lexi did, but they sure loved to repeat the excuse.

Matt sighed heavily. "We have to or it would starve."

"You could just open a bag of dog food sometime," Diego suggested.

"You would think, wouldn't you?" Matt said, giving Lexi a pointed look.

The table erupted into laughter, drawing attention from other patrons and finally, the waitress, who gave a look of surprise and hurried over. "You slipped in here when I wasn't looking."

Shane smiled. "I knew you'd find us when you had time." She had to be seventy if she was a day, and she was as much a fixture of the place as the chrome, red vinyl, and checkerboard floor.

"You, I found. Time, I'm still looking for," she said, giving him the same look his grandma had laid on him years ago when he'd eaten an entire apple pie she'd left out to cool. "What can I get you?"

He glanced at Caitlin. "Burger and a shake? You'll never have one better."

"Sounds great," she said.

"My usual times two," he said, a little too pleased that they liked the same food, because it didn't matter. At least, it shouldn't. And it wouldn't in a few days, because he'd be gone.

"I can open dog food," he heard Lexi say. Were they *still* on that?

"He just won't eat it," Matt said. "He doesn't trust anything she puts out for him."

Despite the jab, Lexi laughed, and Shane wondered why those two couldn't see what was right in front of them.

His gaze skated to Caitlin and back. "But," he said, "*the dog* will cross a bridge with her, which is more than I can say for Caitlin."

She stiffened next to him, suggesting he probably shouldn't have brought that up again.

Lexi confirmed as much when her eyes widened. Incredulous, she asked. "*You're* the woman from the bridge?"

• • •

And there it went. Anonymity busted. Reputation established.

"You have no idea how much I want to say no to that," Caitlin responded, almost certain her face flamed neon. Despite her dedicated status as an introvert, she'd immediately liked Shane's friends. Apparently button-pushing was a thing between them, and a heck of a lot more entertaining when she wasn't the target.

"Don't give it a second thought," Lexi said. "I hate that bridge. It shakes when you walk over it, which in no way convinces me it's safe."

Relief wedged through the embarrassment. "It actually moves?" Caitlin asked Lexi. "I thought that was me being terrified."

Lexi shook her head. "I'm not kidding. I will not walk

over that bridge."

"Seems you're in good company then," Jack said. He followed with a warm smile toward Caitlin.

Lexi shot him a glare anyway. "But she met Shane, so it's all good."

Caitlin rolled her eyes. "Yes. Trying to get away from him was exactly how I got off the bridge."

The group fell silent for a long, unnerving moment. Long enough for her to realize they couldn't possibly know she was joking, before Diego said "daaaaaaamn" under his breath and they started laughing again.

"That was a prime example of my exemplary skill as a first responder," Shane said. "Do you have any idea how much it takes to get a woman to voluntarily walk away from me?"

"Caitlin looks unimpressed," Jack said, "so I'm guessing not much."

Lexi pressed splayed fingertips to her chest, like she couldn't believe her ears. "You mean you didn't swoon and fall at his feet?"

Caitlin shook her head and brushed a crumb off the table. "No, but I can tell I'm an exception."

"Smart woman," Matt said. "Especially considering he's bailing on us for a more prestigious gig in another city."

He was leaving? Was that why he wasn't interested in her? She blinked. "That's good to know. I'm not sure how much longer I would have been able to hold out. Hard to resist a guy who spends hours reading books about the history of childbirth while drinking cinnamon roll coffee out of a mug that professes the difficulties in getting a man."

"I will pay you a *thousand* dollars for a picture of that," Diego said while Jack choked on his drink.

"*If* that had happened," Shane said, "and I'm not saying it did, I can assure you there would be no photos."

"However, the *security* footage…" Caitlin added, biting

back a grin when Shane gave her a look of alarm. Good. He deserved to be thrown off-balance. She just wished she knew why she had been. So what if he was leaving? She'd asked him to do so a dozen times, and now she couldn't even bring herself to ask for details.

The waitress arrived with their food in paper-lined plastic baskets, which momentarily drew everyone's attention back to their meals while Caitlin gawked. The burger looked amazing, but what she couldn't get past was the fluted, frosty mug piled high with thick swirls of whipped cream topped with a cherry. A candy-striped straw added the finishing touch.

Though he didn't say anything, Shane's gaze rested on her when she tried it, and had most likely remained when her eyes rolled back in her head.

Heaven.

This, she'd cross ten bridges for.

Shane grinned at whatever expression she'd just made, and despite the crowded room, the gesture felt intimate.

"How are things going at the bookstore?" Diego asked, dragging her from the spell she was under.

"Warm without an air conditioner," Caitlin managed to say with a sheepish grin. She only vaguely recognized Diego from the air conditioner episode—he'd been in his full gear when he'd given them a hand with the fans—but she figured they'd all been there if they were on Shane's shift. "Thanks for not hosing the place down."

"I'm glad we didn't have to," Jack said. "Pretty cool to have an independent bookstore in town, so I'm glad to see you here to rescue that old place. When are you going to open it up?"

"If I can keep the fire department away"—she shot a pointed look at Shane—"then as soon as I get through enough of the inventory."

"Forget that," Matt said. "I want to know how you're

getting to work. Or did I sleep through the excitement on the scanner?"

Yep, she wouldn't live this down any time soon. "The guy in the shop next door told me about Uber. I'm not sure why Shane couldn't have mentioned that option."

"Some men have to be creative to get that second date," Lexi said.

"Third," Shane tossed back. "She couldn't get through a single day without me."

"But wouldn't I like the chance," she threw out, not bothering this time to correct the not-a-date thing.

Noticing that Shane didn't, either.

"You'll get it," Lexi said. "Apparently Denver holds an appeal we just can't match here. Greener pastures and all."

"More like grayer pastures," Matt said.

"Concrete, even," Diego added.

"None of us want him to go," Lexi told Caitlin, shooting a scowl at Shane.

Matt titled his head in Jack's direction. "Except him. I think he's up for promotion."

Jack held out his hands in defense. "I don't want his job. Besides, that happens and I have to stay out of trouble. Instead of helping them TP his truck, I'm going to be the victim."

"Damn straight," Diego said.

"I don't know what you're talking about," Matt said at the same time.

Shane shook his head. "All three of you need a good run-in with karma."

Jack shrugged. "Don't park next to the sprinklers."

"A fire hose is not a sprinkler," Shane argued.

"Annnnd we're back to men and their hoses," Lexi said, rolling her eyes. To Caitlin, she said, "I'm glad you're here. Don't abandon me."

Lexi didn't have other friends who would kill to hang out

with these guys? No non-awkward way to ask that question, but Caitlin's surprise must have shown.

"Matt and I hang out a lot, though most of the time I'm not sure why, because I'm never going to get a date with him following me around, and these men travel in a pack. No woman wants to put up with them," Lexi explained.

"Except you," Shane reminded her.

"We are mutually and *completely* friend-zoned. I haven't seen another woman come within twenty feet of you guys without someone trying to hook up, and frankly it's just too much to keep up with."

Jack snort-laughed. "Way to keep Caitlin from abandoning you."

"Well, no, there's hope," Lexi argued. "Because none of you are going to mess with the lieutenant's girl, and he's leaving in two weeks, and not even he can screw up so badly in two weeks that she won't want to look at us again."

The *lieutenant's girl*? "Um, I'm not his…" *Anything*. "We're just friends." If they were even that.

"Doesn't matter. He saw you first," Lexi said, toying with the straw in her glass. "Bro code. They'd never break it."

The group shot assessing stares at Shane, which was fantastic, because that meant none of them noticed how flaming red Caitlin's face must be.

Almost none. Because Shane was too close to miss it.

And there wasn't a chocolate shake in the world that could make her forget the look in his eyes when he noticed and grinned.

Chapter Seven

Shane was out of his league. Even though the guys were somewhat surprisingly on their best behavior, right up until they'd abandoned the table seconds after declaring Caitlin *his girl*, there was no way they hadn't noticed the way he noticed her. Sitting next to her had been a mistake. He should have told her to move in next to Lexi…so he could gawk across the table. Yeah, that wouldn't have worked.

Every time Caitlin's mouth closed on that straw, his pants got tighter.

And he had to ride a motorcycle home.

His grin widened. Wouldn't Caitlin just *love* that?

Only one way to find out.

"I've proved harmless enough," he said, trying hard to seem innocent and causal when he had nothing but nefarious thoughts running through his mind, the least of which involved finding out if her lips were as soft as they looked. If she put *half* the passion into him that she did worrying, he'd be in for a hell of a night. "Why don't you let me give you a ride home?"

Caitlin glanced around, probably looking for an ally in Lexi, but the woman in question stood across the room, next to a pinball machine, involved in an animated dispute with Matt. Shane was surprised how quickly they'd made their excuses and cleared out, but he recognized it for the gesture it was. In the meantime, Lexi had just given Matt an elbow in his side that put him against the wall two feet away. Leave it to the two of them to kill each other over an arcade game.

With a look of suspicion he deserved, whether or not she knew as much, she said, "I've been on enough bridges with you today, thanks. I'll call someone. Or app them. Whatever you're supposed to say."

No way he'd let her get away with that. Maybe she was right and he really did harbor a gnawing need to play the hero, but he wasn't ready to let her go yet, either. The least he could do was get her home, and maybe not think about her sliding naked between the sheets after he got her there. "As your companion who is not a date, I'd like to know you made it back safely. Please. I promise to take the center lane. What Uber guy would do that?"

"Most, I'm guessing, if you asked nicely." Her tone still bore suspicion, not that he could blame her.

"And if I ask nicely?" He hated how much he wanted her to agree.

She sighed. "Fine. As long as you promise to take the center lane and not stop on the bridge."

"I hereby promise all of those things." He withdrew his wallet and threw down a few bills. They needed to get out of there, because if she didn't quit sucking on that straw he was going to explode. Especially since for some godforsaken reason all he could picture was her in that button up shirt and messy bun, down on her knees, unzipping his pants, glasses ever so slightly askew—

"You guys done here?"

He blinked at the waitress, who'd just dragged him out of a world of trouble…not that he was entirely grateful. "We are," he said, "but the rest of the gang will be back, so don't kick them off the table just yet. You know they're good for it."

She gave a weary sigh that bore the weight of a long day on her feet. "I know. Best tippers in town."

He grinned. "Best waitress."

She swatted at him. "Stop flirting with me in front of this lovely young woman. You're going to run her off before you ever get your foot in the door."

"The door is firmly closed," Caitlin said, flashing another one of those infuriatingly delectable saccharine smiles.

"It's about time someone didn't make it easy for him," the waitress said with a laugh. "Enjoy your night, even though I think she just indicated that won't happen quite the way you want."

"I have my ways," he said, earning a bemused glance from Caitlin.

She waited for the waitress to leave before clarifying her terms, no doubt a response to his declaration. "If you think you can stop implying you have any chance with me whatsoever," she said, "and will also not drive near the edge of the bridge, I'll let you take me to my driveway."

He barely heard her list of demands, mainly because he'd gotten caught up in watching her mouth move. "Hey, I'm good for my word." He stopped, realizing what she'd said. "Only the driveway? I can be trusted all the way to the front porch. Possibly beyond."

"That's what I'm afraid of," she said under her breath.

He didn't ask what she meant. Ignorance, just this once, might be bliss. Because if he and Caitlin were on the same page, he was in a world of trouble.

He caught Jack's eye and gave him a bro nod to indicate they were leaving so someone would know to reclaim the table, then followed Caitlin through the packed diner. The place was awesome, vintage to the core, and offered some of the best food he'd ever had in his life.

But none of that compared to the moments after Caitlin Tyler had walked with him through that door and sat by his side in his favorite booth. He wasn't supposed to be this crazy about her. Especially not when she presented such a challenge. But already, his mind had gone to what all that passion and power-playing might do to a fresh set of sheets, and…hell, he might as well give up trying to walk around her.

Outside, the fresh air did little to clear his head.

"So," she said. "You're leaving town."

"Yeah. Which is what makes me your ideal date. Or, not date." He'd forgotten their deal, and suddenly he didn't like the terms. A date wouldn't be the worst thing, though maybe the line she'd drawn was for the better. This was new territory for him, wanting something he couldn't have, and keeping his distance would be the smart thing to do.

Unlike plotting to have her cling to him while she straddled his bike.

They walked in silence, the chorus of the city a backdrop. He'd parked a couple of blocks over in the municipal lot, which saved him from the annoyance of a parking meter and not so much the awkward aftermath of having his friends declare her *his girl*.

"Where are we going?" she finally asked when he led her to a side street.

Though it was as well lit as anywhere else, the old lantern-style streetlights that lined downtown had been replaced by plain, utilitarian ones. The landscaping, which consisted of hardy blooms and indigenous grasses, had whittled down to bare concrete with the occasional mulched tree. It would have seemed perfectly clean and kept if not for the curated beauty on display everywhere else. As it were, he didn't blame her for being wary, though it irked him that she remained wary of him.

However good her reasons, not that *she* knew them yet.

"There's a lot over here for city employees, mostly for daytime use, but it works," he said. "I'm not a fan of meters."

They walked up on a squirrel, and she watched it take off across the bare parking lot before questioning Shane. "I'm not allowed to be afraid of that death span, but you can avoid parking meters?"

"I didn't say I was *afraid* of them." He paused next to the bike, though he wasn't sure she'd noticed it. Instead she watched him, so he leaned close to whisper against her ear, "If your pulse never kicks up over 60, you're barely breathing. Get out there, Caitlin. Live a little."

He backed away a bit, though her face remained inches from his. Alone on that side street, the sounds of the city faded. Moonlight bathed the warm evening.

And her.

He'd never seen anyone so beautiful. His logical side tried to pinpoint it—the brightness of her eyes or the softness of her mouth, or maybe the way her hair splayed so wildly on a woman who was afraid to cross a damned four-lane bridge— but instead of an explanation, all he got was a rush. Need crawled through him, bringing with it the crippling desire to touch her mouth. Whether he dragged his thumb across her full lower lip or dipped his head and gave into the craving to kiss her, that touch would haunt him.

But no more so than she would, a hint of a smile teasing the corner of her mouth as she watched him. He couldn't help feeling like it was an unspoken challenge.

One he wanted to accept.

Instead, he took a full step back, accidentally nudging the bike.

Her gaze shifted and her eyes flew wide. "You've got to be kidding me."

The intensity of the moment faded, and he wondered if it had just been him. Imagining her breathless would do that to a man. He glanced from her to the bike, then decided imagining her straddling anything wasn't much better.

Damned lucky machine.

He recognized the tension that had her limbs tight and face blanched, but he dodged the guilt and instead grabbed the moment for all it was worth. "What's the matter?" he asked, feigning innocence. "You scared?"

He'd learned her body language the first time on the bridge, and yeah, she absolutely was scared, but he caught a hint of determination when she flexed her hand out of a fist and straightened her spine. She set her mouth into a haughty smirk that he'd have given his right arm to kiss off her lips and crossed her arms across her chest in an unmistakable gesture of defiance.

"If you think you can handle us both at once," she finally said, "I'd love to see you try."

. . .

Shane's response to Caitlin's challenge was to swing his leg over the bike and offer her a helmet. She stared at the proffered protective gear and wondered what good it would do the rest of her. Forget being plastered to the pavement... she had a much bigger concern, and that was holding on to him. There'd been enough crowd-necessitated body contact in the diner to leave her on a very achy edge — one she'd certainly go over if she had to sit behind him on that bike. He'd *literally* be between her legs. Ninety percent of her hesitation rested with that point, not that she'd admit it.

"You having second thoughts about being handled?" he asked, treating her to that smirk she'd once thought cocky. Now, she wondered how it tasted, and how quickly she'd wipe it off his face if she made a move to find out.

Hell yeah, she was having second thoughts about being *handled*.

"No," she lied, taking the helmet. She slid it on while he did the same, then she hesitated. How, exactly, did a person climb onto one of those things? Turning her back on him and walking away sounded like a better idea with every ticking second, but when he held out his arm, she somewhat grudgingly accepted. So what if she rapidly approached the point where she'd rather face that bridge than her attraction for him? He was leaving. Between that and the fact that he was a trained medic, she didn't have much to lose, at least when it came to bridge crossings.

She'd worry about the rest later.

Like how little difference there was between casual contact with his hand and touching her tongue to a 9-volt battery. Or how strong he had to be to so easily hoist her onto the seat behind him. She tried to keep her distance, but with a backward tug, he managed to lodge her tightly against his back.

Breath *whooshed* from her lungs. Her thighs hugged his. She'd seen enough television to know her upper body was supposed to follow suit. Tentatively, she moved her arms forward to his sides. Electrical tingles fired everywhere they touched.

"All you need to do is stay with me," he said. "Lean the same way I lean, and you'll be fine as long as you hold on."

With virtual fireworks blinding her to everything but the damning strength and heat of his body against hers, he couldn't have been more wrong. Everything was not going to be fine. She was going to lose her grip on *something*, and with any luck it would be him. He could dump her in the parking lot and she'd find her way back to the town square.

Where the milkshakes were.

Then she'd be fine.

He fired up the bike, startling her to the point that she

almost fell off before they'd moved an inch. The noise and vibration had her locking her arms around him in fear, but all thoughts of survival flew straight back toward lust when her fingertips rested on his abdomen. He was a *rock*. That soft tee felt like her favorite sheets, which did nothing to keep her thoughts out of the bedroom, but the muscles beneath it were the kind best seen in sweaty, low-light photos, where shadows threw light over every ridge and ripple and—

The bike lurched.

She bit back a screech before realizing he'd only walked it forward a couple of inches. "Wanted to make sure you were paying attention!" he yelled over the roar.

The words vibrated deliciously in his chest, spreading a tingle from her fingertips to her core, which already tingled thanks to straddling both him and the leather seat.

"Just get it over with," she muttered. She gripped his shirt, not caring one bit if she stretched it out in knots, because clinging to his abs would not end well.

He kicked off against the pavement. The roar she expected didn't materialize. The speed felt more like coasting, and the traffic was sparse enough to waylay her fears of playing speed bump to a jacked-up Ford. She tensed every time the bike jolted, but overall, the whole riding-a-motorcycle-with-a-hot-guy thing wasn't bad.

For about five minutes.

Everything changed when they neared the bridge. What had been a pleasantly warm evening turned chilly with the sudden river-driven blast of cold air, and without buildings to block the wind, all she could think was that she was about to be blown off into the water sloshing murderously in the river bed.

He made an easy turn, then yelled, "Hold on."

She traded her grip on his shirt for an actual embrace. If she was going down, it wouldn't be alone.

As soon as her hold tightened, he gunned it.

Bright lights flew by in a blur, their reflections skidding across the distant water like living art, but it wasn't the view that left her gasping.

It was exhilaration.

She didn't feel the bridge shake or hear the rush of the water. The motorcycle ate up the pavement, but the moment passed in thrilling slow motion, her senses alive with the scent of whatever laundry detergent he used and the utter warmth of his skin beneath. His muscles flexed as he maneuvered the bike, the ease of his ability to control such raw power the kind of turn on that dragged her thoughts to horizontal positions. Ones that happened between hot bodies and cool sheets.

Ones that definitely shouldn't happen between the two of them. Not that reality killed her fantasies, for which she'd have kicked herself if doing so didn't greatly increase the likelihood of scraping the pavement.

To her disappointment, he slowed on the other side of the bridge, then steered straight to her house. She hadn't given him her address, so there was no reason she shouldn't find his sense of direction presumptive, if not creepy, but rather than being thrilled for the solid ground beneath her feet, she wanted more.

And she *really* wanted to cross that bridge again.

Another confession that would never see the light of day.

He parked on her drive, killed the engine, and eased off the bike, easily dislodging her embrace only to draw her back into full body contact when he helped her off the machine. After she took off her helmet, she saw that he'd done the same, and that his slightly disheveled hair once again had her mind back in a bedroom. She definitely blamed him, but the wrong reasons clamored in her head. It wasn't that he dragged her over the bridge. It was that she'd ridden him—er, *with* him—over one.

He had a curious look in his eyes, like he was trying to

figure her out. Or maybe the pieces were falling into place. Whatever he thought made him smile, and a moment later, do that maddening thing where he brushed her hair out of her face and made her knees buckle.

"Thanks for the ride," she managed. "And the walk. And dinner."

The more she stumbled over her words, the more disarming that grin. Her gaze dropped to his mouth before she realized that was the mother of all bad ideas. She shouldn't stand three inches from a man and look at his mouth, because despite any rumblings from her inner feminist, that practically begged for a kiss.

A sane, normal person with an ounce of perseverance would have stepped away, but she just stood there. In the longest moment in the history of moments, she rationalized that he blocked her escape, but she wasn't all that into getting away.

"You're welcome," he said.

"I guess I'll, uh…maybe not see you then." Please, no. Because she couldn't fathom why she'd have to call the fire department next, but she had no interest in finding out. "Have a safe trip to Denver."

"I'm walking you to the door," he said.

Great. Now she was headed for her second awkward good-bye moment in all of three minutes. Not even she, the queen of all awkward moments, would have anticipated that. Of all times to become an overachiever, she'd nailed it.

On her porch, she fumbled with the key but managed to get the door unlocked. "Thanks for the ride," she said. "It didn't suck."

"Good," he said. "Because I don't think it sucked, either."

His agreement caught her off guard, and she looked at him in surprise. She'd known how close he stood, so she shouldn't have been startled to find his face inches away. He'd done that in the parking lot, completely out of nowhere, his lips grazing her ear. It still burned from his touch, and if that crackling of lust didn't calm itself, she'd willingly become the next Van Gogh in her effort to escape it. Tangling anything of hers with anything of his was on her nope list, so for her gaze to once again drift to his mouth meant nothing.

Until his lips touched hers.

Honest-to-God sparks lit the sky. She went numb, all except the party happening on her lips. Every bit of her hard-won resistance shattered, and the stark reality that her bed was the only thing she'd wholly unpacked went screaming through her head. It was the longest brushing-of-lips in the history of human copulation, and she'd have wallowed naked in it if she could.

Walking away would have been a much better idea, but she hadn't exactly batted a thousand on those lately. The only thing she'd managed consistently since she arrived in Dry Rock was to stumble into one awkward moment after the next, each and every one witnessed by the fire lieutenant. And now here she stood, wanting him, and there was no way it wasn't obvious. Seriously, what the hell?

It had just been a simple kiss.

They parted by millimeters, and she whimpered, the moment hanging heavily between them for a split, indecisive moment.

Then it exploded.

With a groan, he grabbed the back of her head and captured her, pulling her mouth to his, tasting and teasing, driving a spike of need through her that left her falling deeper, drowning in something that made rafting through a class five rapid seem sane. She clung to him as he pulled her close, voicing a quiet verse of profanity that made her want to beg him to come inside.

Again and again he drove the kiss while she clutched uselessly at his shirt, drawing him deeper, burning for more.

Wanting everything.

He tasted amazing. He moved like a god. He…let her go. Their eyes met, and she could have sworn through her own lust-filled haze that he was doing a little drowning of his own. But then he straightened and stepped back, and the cocky hero facade was on.

While she stood there, dazed and unblinking, he threw back a careless grin and said, "Hey, how about bringing that book by the station for my next shift? I kinda liked it."

He didn't wait for a response.

Just walked back to the bike, threw his leg over, and left her standing in shambles on her unfamiliar front porch while he roared off into the night.

She stared after him until he was gone, and long after that. What was she *doing*? She didn't just kiss guys on her porch. She barely knew him, and now she'd wanted to drag him to her bed? The man was supposed to put out fires, not set them. And she…she wasn't sure what happened when she got close to him, but she couldn't afford to get burned.

She thought of the card he'd given her with his name and number. It would be so easy to pull it out and shoot him a text. Despite his determination to annoy her at every turn, she'd bet he'd come right back over for a drink, and if not, the rejection contained to the screen of her smartphone would be the easiest possible letdown. But that wouldn't do anything to waylay her need to clench her thighs together.

If anything, it'd be worse.

So much worse.

She closed the front door and withdrew the card from her bag. And then she did the only thing she could if she was going to survive the next two weeks with him in Dry Rock.

Throw it in the trash and leave it without a backward glance.

Chapter Eight

Shane knew he was going to catch hell when he showed up for his next shift. He'd actually expected more of that from the guys at the diner, but they'd held back. Probably because Caitlin was new to town, but more likely because they wanted a read on the situation.

And whatever they thought they'd seen worth reading, they were dead wrong.

Not that that would change anything.

He had a mouthful of a bacon and egg-white concoction Matt had put together on an English muffin when it started.

"Not cool to get involved with her when you have one foot out the door," Matt said. "Now none of us get a chance."

Shane took his time chewing, appreciating the attempt at humor despite the fact that it didn't hide that Matt was calling him out for being a jerk. "As if you had a chance anyway," Shane finally threw back, though without taking his attention from the Formica tabletop. Actually, he was surprised *he'd* had a chance. Most of the women he dated were…compliant. Caitlin seemed to enjoy driving him nuts, and a rejection would have been right up there. Not that they were dating, much less out of rejection territory.

But that kiss. Goddamn. It was all he could do to get out of there, and then he'd spent the whole night awake, thinking about going back. Wondering if she'd actually stop by to see him, then deciding he was crazy for thinking she'd consider it. He'd caught her off guard, and unless he managed to forget that hold she'd had on his mouth and every touch that went along with it, he'd be paying for that for a long time to come.

If he knew her at all, she'd see to that.

"You don't know I didn't have a chance," Matt said. He wiped his hands on a dishtowel and went back to the bacon. While on shift, they all took turns with dinner and were mostly on their own for lunch, but Matt usually took the helm at breakfast. No one knew why, nor did they complain. Anything hot was better than granola or cereal...unless it was something Lexi fixed. That woman had actually ruined PBJ—and to some extent, an entire departmental picnic—an extraordinary feat which in itself was the extent of her talents in the kitchen.

Shane measured his words. As long as Lexi was in the picture, he doubted a bus full of swimsuit models would turn Matt's head, but Matt would be the last person on earth to admit it. He settled for neutrality. "I don't know the last time you went out on a date, so don't blame your drought on me. And on that note, what the hell is on this sandwich? Who has bacon and egg white in one place?" Egg whites, he thought, were for health nuts. Bacon was...bacon. Not exactly a match made in heaven, at least if you were the type to dispute a yolk.

"And butter," Diego added, catching the conversation as he walked through the door, the napkin in his hand all that was left of his own breakfast sandwich. "It's all over the English muffin."

"It's not just egg white," Matt said dryly. "You may have

noticed the yolk is smaller and tends to be in the middle, surrounded by the white. Perhaps if you took a man-sized bite?"

"He's been watching Food Network again," Jack cut in with a laugh. He'd walked in behind Diego, both having beaten Shane to the breakfast table and cleared out before he settled in. Shane wasn't normally last in, but then again, he didn't normally spend a few extra moments staring at himself in the mirror, wondering if his mouth looked as different as it felt. None of his paramedic training explained the weird tingling that lingered on his lips long after he'd left Caitlin on her doorstep.

"He did have a date last night," Jack said. "He's probably worn out."

"If you say what I think you're about to say," Shane warned, "I'm going to put you on the floor." He may have entertained a few dozen thoughts about what he'd wanted to do to that woman, but if any of them voiced a single one, he'd follow through on that threat before they finished the first sentence.

Jack gave him an incredulous look. "You want to beat me up because I think you hurt yourself begging?"

Like hell that was what he meant, but Shane let it go. "I didn't beg," he said, "because it wasn't a date."

Diego snorted. "Note the implication that he does beg on actual dates."

"Don't you have an engine to wash?" Shane asked, trying not to glare. He didn't have a thing with Caitlin, and he knew they were just kidding around, but something fiercely protective clawed at him, and he wasn't sure what to do with it.

Diego and Jack scattered.

Shane stuffed half the sandwich in his mouth so he could ignore whatever Matt was about to say.

Naturally, he said it anyway. "Don't you think it's fucked up to get involved with her when you're leaving?"

Shane took his time chewing. And swallowing. "I'm not involved," he finally said. "And it's not her concern where I go. As long as she doesn't forget how to call dispatch, her odds of survival are the same whether I'm here or in Denver."

Solid argument, he thought.

Matt apparently disagreed. "I've seen you look at a lot of women in the last few years, and I don't think I've seen you look at one like that."

Shane toyed with his food. He wasn't convinced he'd looked at her in any kind of way, though he had to admit—if only to himself—that she was different. No one before her had made him feel this way, which didn't make it deep or monumental, but damned if he wasn't struck by it anyway. "We had to rescue her twice in less than six hours. It's self-preservation."

With a knowing look, Matt said, "Yeah, I think I'd call that the opposite of self-preservation. Maybe you should stick around and see where it goes. It's not like Denver is going anywhere."

The suggestion was deceptively casual, but it hit a nerve. Shane did a half-ass job of tamping down his irritation. "Yeah, but I am. Period. I've done what my mom wanted, or my sister wanted, most of my life. This is for me, and it's long overdue." Too long. What had started as a guilt-driven nicety had taken control of his life, and he wanted it back. "As for what is or isn't going on with Caitlin, I'll tell you what, Matt. You admit you've got a thing for Lexi and we'll talk. Until then, you're the last person to call BS."

Matt stared for a moment before shaking his head and walking off.

Shane studied his sandwich. Damned if the thing didn't have a yolk after all. He finished it in one large bite and rinsed the dishes Matt hadn't gotten to yet, then headed out after the rest of the guys. The line about the engine hadn't been an excuse. The equipment had to be washed every morning, which tended to suck in the dead of winter, but it wasn't so bad during the warmer months.

He found his gaze drifting toward the bridge and the neighborhoods beyond. He hadn't spoken to Caitlin since he'd left her standing on her porch, staring after him in shock. He'd been grateful then for the chance to turn his back and throw on a helmet, because that kiss was supposed to put that irritated fire in her eyes, not send him into a tailspin at the thought of her little whimper. She'd probably forgotten all about it, whereas he'd spent the last thirty-six hours thinking about nothing else.

She must have gotten to work the day before. Probably this morning, too, though it was still early. She had Uber and a footbridge under her belt, besides which, she was a grown, capable woman. She would cross the bridge a thousand times without him, and he'd be gone without a second thought, so he wasn't sure why he couldn't stop thinking about her.

Which was probably why he didn't see it coming when the first blast of water hit him in the chest.

He sputtered.

Matt hit the ground laughing.

Jack stood to the side, hands out in a gesture of innocence he didn't quite sell, but he obviously wasn't the one controlling the spray.

Which only left one.

Diego peered nearly hidden from behind the engine, a telltale pool forming at his feet. Shane hid a grin. The leaking nozzle gave it away every time.

"Better sleep with your eyes open," he warned to thin air, a whopping millisecond before the next blast hit.

But this time he wasn't blindsided. He launched, slinging

himself around the corner of the truck with a one-armed grab that sent him flying at Diego with warp-like speed.

Diego took aim again, but Shane managed to spin the nozzle on him, the brunt of the spray missing them both.

"Oh—!"

At the sound of a woman's voice—*Caitlin's voice*—Shane and Diego both let go of the hose at once. It hit the ground with a plop, landing directly on the handle and spurting a final stream of water directly up into Shane's face.

"Ah, hell, I'm sorry," Diego said—not to Shane, but to Caitlin—and Shane had never believed him more. He'd never seen anyone look more horrified, except maybe Caitlin herself.

Still half blinded, he wiped the moisture from his face with his wet forearm. Not the most effective tactic, considering all he did was move it around, but it was enough to give him a slightly less water-blurred view of Caitlin, who stood at the edge of the meticulously landscaped lawn, staring down at her wet white shirt, a water-splattered paper coffee cup in each hand.

"Go grab one of my off-duty shirts," Shane called over his shoulder to Matt.

"Really sorry," Diego repeated, before adding, "and for the record, not looking."

Yeah, she'd just won every wet T-shirt contest in existence. No way Diego had missed *that*. "If you hadn't looked," Shane snapped, "you wouldn't know not to look now."

"Well, I'm *not* looking now," he said dryly, "so that counts for something."

"It would be great if *no one* would look," Caitlin said.

Not a damned chance, Shane thought, but did his best to avert his gaze from tight dark nipples easily visible through the shirt and the bra underneath. At least two parts of her were cold, and he felt like an ass for standing there thinking of how he'd like to warm them up with his mouth.

"Here you go," Matt said behind Shane.

Shane took the shirt, grateful for the distraction. "Thanks, man." He settled the fabric over Caitlin's head, then relieved her of the cup she held in each hand. She was probably freezing. It was a nice day, but not exactly warm enough to compensate for being drenched with cold water.

Her bright green eyes dug into him as she shrugged into his tee. It hung large on her, and immediately gained wet boob prints, but at least it wasn't transparent. She used the bottom end to wipe water off her glasses then settled them back in place. "I brought you the book," she said, digging into the bag he'd failed to notice, but now peeked from under his shirt. "And one of those is yours."

"You brought me coffee?" It was so…domestic. And also quite possibly the most casual gesture on the planet, so he needed to stop reading into it.

"Yes. Black. I figured anything you might want to add to it would be stocked in the kitchen here, and that flavored stuff didn't seem to be working for you."

Her words took him aback. To be honest, he hadn't expected her to show up with the book, and if he'd harbored a guess, he'd figure she'd pitch it at his head before handing it to him nicely, much less alongside a gift of coffee. Especially since she'd already admitted she'd considered they had coffee at the station, not to mention had already figured out he wasn't as into cinnamon-roll flavoring as he may have led her to believe. To that point, he asked, "What made you think I wasn't a fan?"

"You kind of wrinkled your nose going in."

"It was new." And also not good. She'd nailed him there, but he didn't need to make it easy for her.

"Every sip?"

He laughed, though inwardly he cringed. The woman

could already read him, but hell, she'd *bothered* to read him. "You watched every sip?"

Her cheeks turned pink. "Yours is the one with the X on it," she said, completely ignoring his question.

He inspected the cups then handed hers back to her. "May I assume I'm forgiven?"

She dug the book out of the bag and handed it to him. "Now that you've admitted you did something in need of forgiveness? Probably not."

"Hey, that was a cheap shot."

Her brow rose. "And soaking me with a water hose?"

"That was *Diego's* cheap shot," Shane protested.

She shrugged. "I'm pretty sure you were in there, but either way, *Lieutenant*, it's your shift. Aren't you supposed to make them behave?"

"Probably, but they're restless, not having to escort you across the bridge this morning. Did you walk?"

She shivered and took a sip of her coffee. "I did not."

"If you ever need a ride, just let me know." He wished he'd given her a better one last night, and currently entertained a less ass-hatted desire to take her to work or wherever she needed to be, because driving her had to be a better option than walking a few blocks in soaked shoes, but he mostly just wanted an excuse to see her.

He wouldn't have many more opportunities for that.

She batted her eyelashes in an obvious bit of mockery. "So you're in it for the whole two weeks, then?"

Ouch. He wished he had a read on the sentiment behind her words. Did she want to see more of him? Or was this another lob of sarcasm, calling him out on what she probably thought to be insincere bullshit. "Yeah," he said. "The entire time."

She pointed at his motorcycle in the parking lot and said, "I'll keep that in mind next time I want my thighs to vibrate all night."

Goddamn. Did she have any idea she was throwing these double entendres? No one could be that innocent, but she didn't look the least bit interested in toying with him. At least not like she had after that kiss. He must be every bit the presumptive jerk she thought he was, because he could have sworn he'd been one bite of her lip away from being invited inside. But what had he done with *that*?

Fled.

And now, he harbored regrets. Raging motherfuckers. "Sweetheart, if you want your thighs to vibrate—"

"If I need a fireman," she said firmly, "I'll call 911."

"If you need one," he all but growled, "you'll call *me*."

"And once you're gone?" She'd said the words as a challenge, like she was finally up for playing his game, but damned if they didn't hit hard. Again.

He sipped his coffee to put off having to answer, but it didn't help. He couldn't shake the attraction, or the uncertainty that followed his every thought of Denver. He knew what he wanted. A high-stakes, high-adrenaline job in a place he was needed. A chance for advancement. His father's legacy.

Women, warm and willing, who wouldn't throw up roadblocks at every turn.

And not one of them would be Caitlin.

She watched him, expecting an answer.

He gave her one that made no sense under any circumstances whatsoever.

"Call me anyway."

Chapter Nine

Caitlin arrived at Shelf Indulgence a full hour after she'd planned, in no small part due to the detour and unexpected shower. But she wasn't hating it. The cold water at the fire station had come as a shock, but she'd salvaged her coffee and her book had remained unscathed. Plus she now had Shane's T-shirt, and she may have taken it off and inhaled through the fabric like she was a starry-eyed teenaged girl, but as there were no witnesses, there would be no admitting that. Not that it was weird. She just happened to like whatever brand of laundry detergent he used. Perfectly normal, non-stalkerish behavior.

Yeah, whatever.

Still, she hoped like hell he'd forget to take it back before he moved.

This morning, like the morning before it, the bridge gave her the good kind of shivers. Memories of clinging to a certain fiercely hot lieutenant who'd been unfazed by a kiss that had nearly dropped her to her knees. Of course, he probably had experiences like that all the time. She'd seen the admiring glances that followed almost every step he took, even lingering on him at the diner.

And the way he hadn't returned a single one of them.

"Shut. Up," she said aloud, then rolled her eyes. Now she was talking to herself.

She drained the last of her now-cold coffee and started a new cup. While it brewed, she assessed the inventory situation. Several boxes towered relatively untouched in the back, but she'd made decent progress on the shelved books. Getting them completely sorted and organized wasn't a pre-launch requirement, but if she wanted anyone to be able to find anything, it would be a good idea. Not to mention, it would be much easier for her to deal with that kind of task before the store opened. With any luck, that would be within a week or two.

A week or two. Shane would be out of her life. No distractions. Just work.

Thoughts of him were still not distracting her a few minutes later when a knock sounded at the door. Caitlin opened it to find Lexi standing there, looking sheepish. "I know you're not open yet, but I thought I'd see if you needed a hand."

Surprised and initially speechless, Caitlin stepped back and gestured for Lexi to come in. It felt a little weird, with Lexi being Shane's friend, but apparently she hadn't been kidding when she said she was glad to meet Caitlin. "That would be fantastic if you're sure you have time," Caitlin said, "but I'm warning you, there's enough dust in here to grow corn. If you have allergies or a general love of non-particulated air, take heed."

"I'm in," Lexi said with exaggerated seriousness. "But only if you have coffee." She pulled back her hair into a long ponytail that glistened even in the low light.

Caitlin had to bite her tongue not to ask what shampoo

she used to get such gorgeous hair, because that wasn't *at all* creepy. Instead, she gestured toward the table at the back of the room and said, "There's a Keurig and a K-Cup for every possible mood. Help yourself to anything you'd like."

"You've just won seventy-five percent of my heart."

Caitlin laughed. "Okay, I'll bite. What's the other twenty-five percent?"

"It's yours as long as you don't make fun of my cooking."

"So I'm guessing Matt will never own that last quarter?"

Lexi gave a disgusted sigh. "Matt will never own *any* quarters."

"Really?" Caitlin didn't try to hide her surprise.

"Really. Shane and Diego and Jack have absolutely nothing better to do than imply otherwise, but that is not happening. We're next-door neighbors, and I might starve without him, and he's been my best friend for as long as I can remember, but those are the only tenuous threads holding us together."

Caitlin choked back a laugh. *Those* were tenuous threads? She'd kill for that kind of relationship "All that and a dog?"

Lexi shook her head, a glint of humor peeking through what was obviously a long-standing point of contention. "Yeah, because apparently I'm not even capable of opening a bag of dog food."

"Yet Matt chose you to co-parent?" Caitlin led Lexi to the coffee supplies. While Caitlin had had to read the directions on how to use the thing, Lexi didn't flinch.

"The dog chose me," she clarified. "Matt adopted him, yet he always goes straight to me. I cannot tell you the extent to which I find this amusing."

Caitlin chuckled and sipped her coffee. "So you guys are staying together for the kids?" she asked with a laugh.

"More like, that's the reason he hasn't changed the locks." She hesitated. "Okay, the truth is, I adore him, but we'll never be more than friends because I don't know what I'd do without him. No way I'd risk crossing that line and ruining things, even in a weak moment when I don't find him completely repulsive. Which I don't, but it's just easier when I convince myself otherwise. But enough about me, because I have questions of my own." Lexi extracted a K-cup from the stash. "Chocolate-glazed donut? This is a thing?"

Caitlin exhaled. She'd been prepared for an entirely different set of questions. Coffee, she could handle. "It's a delicious thing."

Lexi popped the cup in the machine then turned toward Caitlin. "And you and Shane?"

"Definitely not a thing," Caitlin said. "He decided if I didn't face my fear of bridges that I'd be a drain on city resources, so he took it upon himself to play the rescuer. That is the extent of our relationship."

"That and a date," Lexi said, waggling her eyebrows.

"You can call it a date. He called it public service."

Lexi's eyes widened. "He did not."

God, how Caitlin had missed girl time. Her sister hadn't had a brush with downtime in ages, and she and Caitlin's nephew traveled in a pair. Caitlin loved her nephew, but the conversations in his presence seldom ventured beyond toddler talk.

Lexi was a godsend. Especially in this muddled new place where Caitlin hated how much she wanted a certain lieutenant. Throwing up walls when all she wanted was to be thrown against one—preferably naked—was counterintuitive, frustrating, and probably life-saving, but a second opinion couldn't hurt.

Nor could validation. "Yes," Caitlin said. "He did. Apparently I shouldn't be allowed to roam the streets unsupervised."

Lexi leaned a hip against the old wood-plank counter now

cluttered with coffee supplies and a fake blue floral bouquet sitting crookedly in what bore a disturbing resemblance to an urn, complete with dust in the bottom. "There's potential for that to be adorable," Lexi said.

Caitlin shook her head and reached past Lexi to right the flowers. "I know I'm new here, but he doesn't seem the type to be *adorable*."

Lexi shrugged. "But he's not an ass. The women he dates don't trash him on social media after they stop seeing him. He's got to have a redeeming quality or two."

Caitlin's shoulders stiffened before she could stop them, and she hated herself for the reaction, especially when Lexi's brow kicked up a notch. "So he does date a lot?" Caitlin asked. "Why am I not surprised?"

"Actually, he really doesn't. I think he gets bored."

Caitlin sighed. Hell, she practically swooned. Keeping her attraction hidden from Lexi was a battle Caitlin had long lost. Resigned, she asked, "They throw themselves at him, don't they?"

Lexi snorted and picked an invisible piece of lint off a shirt that perfectly matched her eyes. Caitlin, by comparison, could barely coordinate her shirt and pants. "Have you *seen* the man?" Lexi asked.

"I saw him." Her thoughts went back to the diner, where he'd outwardly ignored an awful lot of blatant appreciation from other women. "And I think it's disgusting when women fall at a guy's feet because he's attractive."

"Attractive is the biggest understatement of all time, and if you tell me you didn't notice, I'm walking out and leaving you alone with the dust and the books."

Caitlin didn't doubt that for a minute. "Yeah, I noticed," she said. "He's smoking hot. They all are. There must be a requirement to get in with the fire department here."

"I've thought the same thing for years. And you'd think

hanging out with so much eye candy would be good for a woman, but guess how many guys ask me out when I'm constantly surrounded by stupidly hot men?"

"That's a first-world problem if I've ever heard one," Caitlin said with a laugh.

"Just wait until you get to know them," Lexi warned. She took her coffee from the machine and added creamer. Because that was exactly what chocolate donut coffee needed…a gallon of sweet milk.

"Well," Caitlin said, "this morning Diego and Shane managed to soak me with a water hose. Does that count?"

Lexi sipped her coffee, failing to hide a smile behind the ceramic. "Am I allowed to laugh? Also, what counts is Shane has a clear interest in getting to know you, which is going to keep the others at a respectable distance."

Caitlin left her cup on the counter and headed to the sofa with a box of books. And tried not to think of Shane camped out there, periodically tossing out sex facts. "Ugh. I don't want to join his list of conquests."

Rather than argue, Lexi said, "I don't think he sees you as a conquest."

"What would possibly make you think that?"

She looked up from where she'd begun rifling through a box of books. "He doesn't normally bring his dates to sit with us, for one."

That news came as a surprise, but Caitlin hoped it didn't show on her face. She didn't need to feel better about him. She *needed* to learn to keep her distance. "This would be a good time to mention him grumbling about how he should have taken me somewhere else."

"Either he made an exception, or he was so flustered by you he managed to forget we're *always* there. I win both points. Wow," Lexi said, staring into the box Caitlin had already discovered to be full of books about sex—one of many such collections she'd found there. "*Kama Sutra*. This is my kind of store."

"There are no fewer than ten boxes full of sex books here," Caitlin said, "and for the record, they were here before I was." She hesitated, not really wanting to further the conversation about Shane, but curiosity overtook her. "Have you considered he doesn't see me as anything more than what he said? A public service?"

"Doubtful." Lexi stopped flipping through the book and held it open to an illustration. "Have you ever tried this? It looks painful. Actually," she said with a wink, "maybe you should try that with Shane. See what he's willing to go through for you."

Caitlin stared, horrified. Not at the suggestion, but the fact that her mind had gone straight to picturing it. She opened her mouth to speak but ended up in a coughing fit. "Dust," she finally said through watery eyes.

"Shall I call dispatch?" Lexi asked.

Caitlin abruptly stopped coughing, even though she hadn't been faking it.

"That's what I thought," Lexi said with a grin. "Either way, you were different for him."

"And I just moved here, so maybe he's just being nice."

Lexi closed the book with a *thud*. "You're as stubborn as he is."

"I'm not sure that's a compliment."

Lexi laughed. "Neither am I, but you've done the exact opposite of convincing me you're not interested in him, and I've known him long enough to tell he's definitely liking what he sees." She dropped the *Kama Sutra* back in the box from which it came, then hauled the whole collection over to sit on the sofa with Caitlin. "I don't know. I'm thinking you guys are perfect for each other."

"What could possibly make you think that?"

With a knowing grin, Lexi said, "Hot librarian and gorgeous firefighter…tell me that's not the coupling of a thousand sexual fantasies."

Caitlin blinked. "Did you just say I was hot?"

Lexi waved a hand. "Please, girl. You're stunning." She leaned closer, even though they were the only two in the room. "And besides, what man can resist a woman with an entire store full of sex books?"

Chapter Ten

Shane should have known his request to his mother would bring questions. He just didn't realize it was going to be a family affair.

All over some homemade éclairs.

"I don't understand, honey," his mother said. She stood in her sunny kitchen, an apron over her dress. She'd worn a dress every day for as long as he could remember. "Aren't you off tomorrow?"

"Yes, he is." His sister, Jess, gave him a measured, somewhat accusatory glare over a glass of orange juice. How anyone could drink orange juice with an éclair, he didn't know. As far as he was concerned, that just ruined both flavors.

"Good to know you've grasped the concept of one day on, two off," Shane told her. He gave her a warning glance he immediately regretted. She'd be all over that like a bloodhound. "Speaking of which, shouldn't you be at work?" His sister taught English as a Second Language, floating between the local schools and community college. If she had a schedule, he'd never been able to grasp it, but early on a weekday seemed as good a time as any to be anywhere else.

She rolled her eyes and pushed her dark hair away from her face. "Just because you work twenty-four-hour shifts doesn't mean the rest of us can't have flexible schedules."

"It's eight in the morning."

"So what? I'm working nine to five. Besides, Mom told me she was making éclairs. Which brings us back to your very special request. The one you never make for your days off."

"It's food. I eat."

"It *is* an unusual request," his mother said, trading glances with her lookalike daughter. How the woman hadn't yet gone gray, he didn't know. At sixty-three, she had the life and energy of someone half her age. Sometimes Shane wondered how losing her husband, his father, hadn't broken her. He still didn't know how she'd been able to move on, away from Denver and the family they'd once been, to start over. Even then, he'd wanted to stay in the shadow of his father's footsteps, to grow up in the only place his family had ever been whole. When he was younger, he thought her ability to put one foot in front of the other meant her heart hadn't been broken, and he'd been pissed. But as an adult, he saw past that. She hadn't dated anyone since. Photos from their marriage adorned the new house as it had the old. His dad's boots still sat by the nightstand, just as they always had. She'd moved on, but she hadn't.

It was the one thing they never talked about.

In that moment, Shane wished those damned éclairs could be another point of avoidance.

"Heard you had another call on the bridge," Jess said. She popped a torn-off bite of éclair in her mouth after she spoke, but it did nothing to hide the smirk.

"It was a misunderstanding," he told her, unsure what information she thought she had, because there wasn't anything to know. Still, she seemed to think she knew something. "A woman who overestimated her ability to cross on foot."

Jess cocked an eyebrow. "How, exactly, does one overestimate one's ability to walk the length of a sidewalk?"

"It happens when you're afraid of rivers and have never crossed a bridge like that before." Damn it, here he was defending Caitlin when he'd had to bite back the same teasing accusation more times than he could count.

Jess picked apart her éclair like she was trying to sell it on an infomercial, squishing the soft dough and dragging a manicured fingertip through the cream filling. "Is that why you took her to dinner?"

There it was. He sighed.

His mother beamed. "You're seeing someone? Here?"

The implication irked him. *Yep, met a woman a few days ago. I'll just dead-end my career now.* "No," he said. "As a matter of fact, other than the fact that my vision is intact, I am not seeing anyone. Especially not here. As you both well know, I report to Denver in a little over a week."

Two pairs of dark, troubled eyes settled on him, mirror images of each other. His mother was the one to speak. "I wish you'd reconsider."

"It's a done deal." The words came out firmer than he'd intended. "And it's my life. It's past time I live it for me." Those words had become his mantra—a go-to when someone questioned why he'd give up "everything" in Dry Rock for a bigger, less personal department. But he didn't see himself wallowing in a bigger pond. He saw bigger opportunities. More room for advancement. Excitement. *That* was what he'd been giving up, and he'd done that long enough.

His mother blanched, but as quickly as she reacted, she shook it off. She wiped her hands on her apron and said, "I'll just go get one of those bakery boxes for you."

Shane didn't watch her go.

If he wanted a knife to twist, he had his sister for that.

Jess's eyes flashed. "You're killing her."

Generally speaking, he adored his little sister, but ever since his transfer had been approved, she'd taken a jab every chance she got. The underlying hurt…he just chose to ignore that. "I think you're exaggerating," he said, "and I cannot base my decisions on a radius someone else dictates. Besides, she said she supported me."

"Of course she *said* that, you moron. But she already lost Dad. Can you imagine how hard it is for her to watch you go try to fill his shoes?"

He thought of all the times as a child he'd done exactly that, stepping into his father's work boots, tripping on the laces while he walked wobbly circles around his parents' bed. "I'm not trying to fill anything."

"You're leaving behind real people to chase a ghost," she said.

He opened and closed his hand, but the exercise did nothing to alleviate the growing tension that clawed at him every time he walked through his mother's door. "I'm getting a promotion."

"At what cost?"

She was on his mom's side, fighting a battle his mother never would. He got that. And he didn't want to hurt either of them, but this was his life, his *dream*, and he wouldn't be guilted out of it. "More of a profit, if you must know, but it's not about that."

She slid off the stool, giving him a brush with hope that she'd give up the fight. "If you're so bent on being the hero Dad was, I think you're forgetting something important."

Wrong. Again. Warily, he asked, "Which is?"

"He didn't leave us because he wanted to, and you won't ever be able to say that."

She slammed her glass in the sink — it was a fucking

miracle the thing didn't shatter on impact—then walked out of the small house that had been the family home for the better part of two decades, though he and Jess had long moved out. He was so lost in thought that he jumped when his mom touched his arm.

"She'll be okay," she said gently. Always gentle, ever the diplomat. Did the woman *ever* say what she really thought?

Guilt besieged him. "Are you?"

She shrugged, but the indifferent gesture didn't keep the shadows from her face. She'd always seemed so happy, which was something else he'd never understood but had come to take for granted. "You love people for who they are," she said. "You can't put conditions on something like that."

"Which is code for?"

This time her smile was genuine. "What is it the kids say now? You do you?"

He laughed. "Where did you hear that?"

"Flora picked it up from her grandchildren," she said of her bedazzled tracksuit–wearing neighbor with Crayola-blue streaks in her hair.

"I can only imagine what she's teaching *them*," he joked, watching as his mom arranged four éclairs in one of the bakery boxes she purchased in bulk and folded the lid. "You know that's overkill, right?"

"Presentation is everything, my boy, and I won't have you taking my pastries out for the world to see in plastic wrap and stained GladWare."

"The whole world, huh?" Actually, it wasn't much of an exaggeration. Steady demand for her baked goods allowed her to retire early from her decades-long job with a floral delivery service after a knee injury made a painful prospect out of getting in and out of the truck all day.

"Not the world," she told him. "Not the fire station, and not that young lady you're trying to impress."

"I'm just returning a kindness," he said, a little too quickly.

His mother *hmph*ed but when she spoke, she'd switched gears. "Follow your dreams. Jess will come to understand a person can't live any other way."

He watched as she leaned down to pet the tabby cat that wound between her ankles. His mother must be having a good day, as far as days went. Sometimes he felt guilty asking her to bake anything, but she insisted it kept her young. Plus, she tended to do it whether or not anyone made a request. "And you?" he inquired. "Are you okay with it?" He hated to even ask. He wanted her to be okay, but what if she said she wasn't? Would he give it up all over again? For so long, he'd let his conscience make decisions for him. He hadn't pushed the transfer, but the time was finally right, and he needed to make his own way whether or not they liked it.

"I know how to buy a bus ticket to Denver," she said.

"Or you could drive your car."

She swatted at him. "I don't drive on the interstate, and you know it."

That, of course, made him think of Caitlin, not that she was far from his mind. He leaned down to kiss his mom's cheek then tucked the box of éclairs under his arm. "I owe you one."

"If I ever start collecting on all those points you claim you owe, you're in trouble."

He laughed, but it didn't quite fill that void that seemed to grow every time the subject of Denver came up with either his mother or sister. But his mom was right. He could cross that bridge a million times and never get anywhere.

Except to Caitlin.

"I'll see you later," he told his mom.

He'd taken his truck. He could have stowed the pastry on the bike and gotten them all there in one piece, but he still hadn't shaken the feel of Caitlin clinging to him. He'd have given just about anything to turn around, to face the other way while she wrapped her legs around his hips and held on, and that was the last thing he needed to think about.

In fact, it was about the only thing he really needed to forget, which did nothing to explain why he was headed over to her shop, pastries in hand, newly prevalent weird feeling in his chest.

He parallel parked in front of her building and caught himself checking his hair in the rearview. *Idiot.* Even if he had ever cared about anything like that, his hair was too short to look anything worse than slightly disheveled. Irritated with himself, he scrubbed his hand through the strands until he managed to make the barest mess of things, and then exited the truck with the éclairs.

He knocked, feeling extremely self-conscious as he waited for Caitlin to open the door. He didn't know for sure she was there, though he couldn't imagine where else she'd be mid-morning.

The door creaked open.

Caitlin blinked with surprise. "Hey."

"Thought you might like to try the best éclairs in town, and I brought back the book."

Her expression shifted to skepticism. "You finished it already?"

"I did." Mostly to be a pain in her ass, but he'd been surprised to find it interesting, if dated. "If there's ever the need for a conversation about what feminists in the nineteen-thirties thought of pornography, I'm your guy."

One sculpted eyebrow rose. "And as a follow-up, you brought me cream-filled, phallic-shaped pastries?"

He snorted laughter. "My mom made those. I can assure you, she didn't have a phallus in mind, let alone a cream-filled one."

"But you do." Her words were cautious. Guarded.

Which told him plenty about where her thoughts had gone, and he wondered if they'd lingered that way for days, as had his. "I do *now*," he said.

And thus descended the most awkward of all silences. He swallowed. "So, Lexi says you have a lot of sex books here."

Yep, the worst possible way to break an awkward silence.

She cleared her throat, only it was more of a cough. Probably even an excuse, but if he'd hoped to open a door, he was sorely disappointed, because rather than invite him to bed—or a lumpy sofa—she oh-so-helpfully said, "And there's a whole section on kittens."

Innocent enough statement, but way too tempting to let go. He waited until she'd taken her first bite before he spoke. "Pussy cats?"

She choked.

He moved closer, just in case he needed to perform the Heimlich maneuver—knowing Caitlin, he'd almost expect it—but she recovered. And glared. "Kittens are perfectly decent. I don't know why you had to do that."

"Yes you do," he said. She had a dab of cream on the corner of her mouth, damn it all. He hadn't considered pastries—even phallic-shaped ones—could turn his thoughts to sex, but there he stood, this beautiful, maddening woman proving that kiss wouldn't be one he'd soon forget. That stupid bit of cream taunted him. Why couldn't she lick it off? Yeah, like *that* would improve the direction of his thoughts.

Hell. Maybe *he* should lick it. A painful tightening of his groin seconded that idea. Before he could act on anything involving his mouth, he reached for her, smearing the cream with his finger.

Her eyes widened, and she turned her head slightly, more of an instinctive reaction than an invitation. After which his finger landed on the middle of her bottom lip. A moment passed, with nothing in the world between them but a few dusty inches of airspace and a really bad idea.

And Denver.

He took a slow, deliberate breath then smudged the cream across her lip. If she bit down on his finger, it was game on. But she found a new method of avoidance. Her eyes drifted closed at his touch, so he took full advantage, studying her face. The way her glasses rested on a smattering of freckles. The length of her lashes. The absolute perfection of her skin.

He tugged at her lip with his thumb.

Her eyes fluttered open.

Denver.

"You have something on your…here," he eventually said, avoiding at all costs the word *cream*, while he coaxed the last little bit from her mouth. He dropped the contact, looked awkwardly at the remnants of her éclair, then gave up and sucked his finger clean, though his mind went elsewhere.

Caitlin watched, her gaze following his hand then shifting to his face. He wondered if she realized what she was doing when she tentatively traced her lips with her tongue, then if she knew what she did to *him*. He would have thought she'd revel in something like that, but she seemed dazed. Unfocused.

They hadn't separated. Not really. He could still smell her shampoo. His finger still tingled with the softness of her lip. "Do you really have a lot of sex books?" he asked.

"Why?" she asked softly. "Do you have a lot to learn?"

He was…impressed. Her tone would have been perfectly at home across a battered pillow sitting cockeyed on a ravaged bed, but she'd landed a jab with expert precision. "I was a little more curious as to what I might learn about you."

Her gaze dropped to his mouth, wrecking him. "I've got news for you, Lieutenant. A book isn't the way to do it."

He took a step back, needing the space. Was she flirting with him? It didn't matter. If he had to report to his new job in the morning, he'd be on the interstate tonight, no matter what she thought of him or sex or anything cream-filled and phallic. Yet… "What about lunch? Tomorrow?"

She left him on edge for the longest time before answering. "I'm sure I'll eat."

"I'll come by at noon," he said, though she hadn't agreed to eating with him. Nor did he give her the chance to say no. Instead, he let himself out of the store, clearing the stoop before he looked back to find her with her fingertips touching her lip and her gaze fixed on him.

He should have called it off right then. Maybe go home and pack a bag or two. Check up on that apartment he'd leased in Denver, even though he'd yet to receive a confirmation that it would be ready on schedule.

But for the first time since the opportunity opened for a transfer, Denver had lost some of its appeal.

And damned if Caitlin Tyler hadn't found it.

Chapter Eleven

Caitlin didn't think she'd ever been as nervous as she was the next afternoon when Shane showed up to take her to lunch. It didn't mean anything. It *wasn't* anything. And even if it was, he was leaving, so it still wasn't.

Damn those butterflies.

And anything cream-filled.

And him. Definitely him. Because her lip still tingled from where he'd touched it, which only reminded her of the kiss she'd tried like hell to forget. And pretty much every moment they'd shared since.

She wanted to ask why he'd invited her, but that only suggested there was a motive, when in reality, he probably just wanted lunch. That she'd spent every waking moment thinking about him didn't mean he'd reciprocated. It definitely didn't mean he wanted her to drag him onto that lumpy sofa and climb on top of him. Naked. In broad daylight. That she wasn't concerned by how her thighs, boobs, or belly would look fully exposed in the aforementioned daylight worried her more than anything.

He stared at her, and she was almost certain he'd read every filthy word of her thoughts. But instead of calling her out on that, he simply said, "I hope you're hungry."

She tugged at her skirt, like an extra inch could protect her from herself, then abruptly let go when she realized thinking of inches wouldn't get her anywhere, either. At least not anywhere she needed to be.

"I might be," she said, then wanted to kick herself because that sounded like bad flirting, and she had zero interest in flirting with him. At least not that she'd admit.

"In that case, can I buy you a milkshake?"

"Yes to the milkshake, but I can pay for myself," she said. Because this was not a date.

His brow rose, but he didn't argue. Which probably meant he wouldn't and would still pay, which meant she'd have to watch him, which meant a whole new brand of trouble. It was bad enough every cell in her body clamored to climb on him. Now she felt obligated to watch his every move, which really wasn't the hardship it should have been.

They walked the handful of blocks to the diner, his fingertips periodically touching the small of her back to navigate sidewalk traffic. The sun beamed, the mountain air the kind of fresh that belonged in a summer lemonade commercial.

"Are you going to miss the air?" she asked, desperately hoping to drag her thoughts from the gutter.

He was quiet for a moment. "There's air in Denver."

"And I bet it smells like exhaust."

"Only if you stand behind a truck," he countered.

"I'm sure it's a bit nicer here." Admittedly nicer even than her hometown in Wyoming. Here, birds sang. Flowers burst from every crevice, and everywhere she looked, she saw color. Back in Wyatt, summers were dry and dusty, the town sepia-toned, like the old westerns her father liked to watch from his recliner on the rare rainy day.

"It's nice here," Shane admitted. "But I've stayed here for most of my adult life, not pursuing what mattered to me, because I worried how it would make my mom and sister feel. I need to be in control of my own life, and what I want is there."

There was absolutely no reason for his words to sting. They should have been a relief, or at minimum something to snap her away from thinking about his mouth and wanting to go back to the moment he'd touched her lips and sucked his finger.

All reasons for her to go back to the bookstore. Alone. Yet, when he held open the door to the diner, she walked in ahead of him.

They greeted the same waitress from their last visit, then he gestured for her to slide into a booth. A smaller, much more intimate booth.

He followed.

Right. Next. To. Her.

Was she supposed to acknowledge that? Or was this just normal here? She glanced around. Other people seemed to be sitting opposite one another. Granted, she had sat next to him the last time, but that was in a round booth that technically had only one long bench. This was—

"What can I get you folks?"

Caitlin asked for a milkshake and a salad. "I ate three éclairs this morning," she explained when Shane gave her an odd look. "Your mother needs to open a bakery. In France."

"I'll have the usual," he said, hiding a laugh, "but double the fries." Then he leaned toward the waitress and said something in a low voice Caitlin didn't quite catch.

The waitress nodded, but she didn't look away from her pad. "Ten minutes," she told them. "I'll be right back with your drinks."

"How's the inventory coming along?" Shane asked when the waitress left. He completely ignored Caitlin's questioning look.

Other than a dozen boxes of sex books? And counting? Yeah, she wasn't going there. "Almost done," she said. "Lexi has been a big help."

"I'm glad you hit it off."

"Me, too, though I can't imagine anyone not liking her."

Shane nodded. "If only Matt would get his head out of his ass and see what he's got in front of him."

Caitlin didn't know them, but she'd heard enough from Lexi that she couldn't help but agree, though the problem was more likely a lack of admission than the lack of anything to admit. "She'd probably just cram it back in for him."

Shane raised his brow. "Sounds like I missed one hell of a conversation."

Yeah, he had. And way too much of it had revolved around him.

The diner was less crowded in the middle of the day, though still doing a robust business. She loved the retro feel of the place, from the black-and-white checkerboard floor to the red-and-chrome seating. Even the music was atmospheric, though it shifted oddly from songs she associated with the fifties to others from the eighties.

"The owner has specific tastes," Shane said after Bruce Springsteen followed Chuck Berry.

"I love it here," Caitlin said. "I'm glad it's within walking distance."

"You ever think of carpooling?" he asked.

"I do carpool."

"I mean without an app."

She shrugged. "You meet people that way."

"I should introduce you to my sister. She'd probably love to check out your store." He paused. "She doesn't teach sex ed, but I'm sure there's something else in there for her."

Caitlin elbowed him.

Sitting on the same side had its advantages after all.

"I have a sister, too," she said. "She didn't want me to move."

"Ditto."

Their food arrived, the salad impressive for a place that served most of their food in baskets. Caitlin noted the freshly grated cheese and springy, crisp lettuce and made a mental note to return every day.

While she gawked at the unlikely bowl of awesome in front of her, Shane picked a fry off a towering mound and dipped it in his shake. "Here," he said, handing it to her. "Try this."

Caitlin stared in mock horror. "You just violated that milkshake."

"Trust me." He took it back, and when she opened her mouth to protest, he popped it in.

Despite being in mid-protest, she briefly closed her eyes. Salty mingled with sweet, hot and crisp with creamy and cool. There had never been a more perfect vessel for fries. "I can't believe I've never tried that," she said.

"It'll never be as good anywhere else. It's the milkshake." He picked up his burger before saying, "Half those fries are yours."

"I can't—"

"They're *fries*. Eat."

She couldn't believe he hadn't suggested a way for her to burn it off. "Fine, but I'm paying."

"Too late. It's already on my tab."

"You cheated," she grumbled, finally realizing what he must have said to the waitress. "You won that round, but I get the tip."

He'd picked up his drink and, with the glass to his

mouth, started laughing. After he made what looked like a monumental effort not to spit it everywhere, she asked, "What?"

"Just say the word, sweetheart, and you'll get the whole thing."

• • •

By the next day, Caitlin had given up trying not to think about Shane. She couldn't begin to label what was going on between them, but whatever it was, she'd never experienced anything like it. She needed to keep her distance, but at the same time, he represented a risk-free probability.

Their days were literally numbered.

She could gawk at his abs all she wanted…there was zero chance they'd go anywhere, so her heart was safe.

The rest of her was another story.

But as far as chances went, he was one worth taking. She did trust him, at least with her fears. She hated how him leaving had become one of them, but she'd face that one soon enough. Alone.

Until then, maybe she could have him, or at least his help. It made sense to ask. If they stayed in public, she'd probably avoid succumbing to the urge to fling herself on him, or the nearest horizontal surface. Not that vertical ones were out, but a girl had to be practical. Wall sex took more coordination than she gave herself credit for having.

So, wall sex aside, she could do this.

Great pep talk.

She stared at the brick station house, which, for the moment, appeared quiet. The bay doors gaped open, revealing an engine, an ambulance, and two other trucks she couldn't readily identify. What she could see of the garage was meticulous. The vehicles gleamed, as did the floor. Her house probably wasn't that clean under all the boxes she'd yet to unpack. Maybe she should just go home and do that. She was crazy for coming back here, and not just because last time she'd been blasted with water.

This time she wanted to ask Shane for help. The thought of doing that left her feeling exposed and vulnerable, which was stupid because he'd gone out of his way to hang out with her.

For public safety.

Which totally explained the kiss.

Frustrated, she blew a stray hair out of her face. The light summer breeze immediately nudged it back in place. She had her face twisted in frustration and an oath spilling from her lips when, several feet ahead, the door to the station swung open and Shane stepped out.

"Hi," she managed.

"Hi. Sorry to interrupt, but the guys were organizing a betting pool over when you'd actually approach the building, and I felt honor-bound to stop—"

"I want to tackle my fear of heights," she blurted. It was either that or ask him to remove his shirt, because surely those abs weren't real. Maybe they were 3D printed. Because *that* was the obvious answer.

A long moment passed before he spoke, and she was suddenly paranoid he'd remained silent for the sole purpose of reading her thoughts. Finally, he asked, "What?"

"Riding across the bridge was thrilling—probably one of the most exciting moments of my life—but I can't walk or drive across, and I don't want to depend on rides from strangers to get to work." The words came in a rush—one designed to keep her from backing out of saying them—but the silence that followed proved uncomfortable.

More so the longer he stared. "I can't imagine they'll be strangers long. There can only be so many Uber drivers in

Dry Rock." His words sounded careful, like he was on the verge of saying the wrong thing. Maybe he was just trying to be polite.

And she was too stupid to let it go. "You just told me yesterday to carpool," she said.

"And you said no."

Heat flooded her face, but she stood a little straighter and blinked back the embarrassment of his rejection. "Okay then," she said. "I should get to the store. Thanks again for… everything."

She turned, incapable of getting out of there fast enough. But she didn't get anywhere. He touched her arm, stopping her in her tracks, and her mind danced back to lunch. To that awkward moment afterward where he'd stood on the stoop in front of the store and she felt sixteen again, wondering if he was going to kiss her.

He hadn't.

Again.

She'd told herself she should still be relieved, but in the face of more disinterest, hurt edged in. Stupid, inexplicable hurt. She might be his type, air breather that she was, but she'd long established a disinterest in him. And, in the dumbest move of all time, she'd forgotten it. Some things were too good to miss, or at least made damning temptations. That had to explain why people lined up for anything limited-edition from Starbucks. Not so much why he so easily dismissed her.

Only, maybe he hadn't. A storm waged in his eyes, drawing her in, twisting her hopes and emotions. Finally, he muttered, "Damn it, Caitlin."

At the same time, she said, "I shouldn't have—"

They fell into a momentary silence, his hand still on her arm, her gaze still locked with his. "I'm on a twenty-four-hour shift," he said, dropping his hold on her without further explanation. "So how about I pick you up at eight tomorrow night?"

"At…at my house?" This sounded way too much like a date. And it would kick off way too close to her bed.

A muscle jumped in his jaw, leaving her to wonder if he'd had the same thought. "Would you like me to get you earlier from the store?"

"No," she stammered. "Eight is fine, thanks." Eight *really* sounded like a date. "But no skydiving."

"I promise not to push you out of an airplane."

"Okay," she said. But was it? There were loopholes in that a person could drive a truck through, but that wasn't what bothered her.

It was the raw intensity in his eyes.

To say nothing of the fact that she'd have to be pushed out of an airplane to ever forget it.

Chapter Twelve

Shane arrived at Caitlin's home promptly at eight the next evening. They had another thirty minutes of daytime left before twilight would settle in, which was just about perfect for what he had in mind.

He stood on her porch and hesitated before ringing the bell, wondering if he'd overdressed by upgrading his usual off-duty jeans and T-shirt. He hadn't gone suit and tie, but the button-up shirt and khaki pants felt like enough of a departure to make him self-conscious. Which only made him feel *more* self-conscious, and that really wasn't a thing he did. At least not with any woman before her.

He pressed the button before he could think too hard about that.

She opened the door quickly. Too quickly. She'd probably stood there watching him, the thought of which would have made him feel even more ridiculous had she not taken his fucking breath.

With a nervous smile, she pulled back her hair, twisting it into her usual messy bun before he could tell her how much he liked it the other way, too. And the black dress that clung casually to her curves and a set of strappy heels didn't detract one bit from that, but hell, she'd look great in a potato sack.

Even better out of it, he'd bet.

"Hey," he said. "You look…" Everything that he could think to say sounded too much like a line. And the blunt truth—that he wanted to remove every stitch of her clothing with his teeth and drive her headboard through her wall—wasn't likely to go over well.

"Unfit for skydiving is what I was going for."

Fuck. Not even those moments of freefall ten thousand feet up had felt like this. "You definitely don't look ready to jump out of a plane." Damned if that wasn't the oddest compliment he'd ever uttered. "Or walk through the woods."

She paused with her hand on the doorframe. "If I'm not jumping out of a plane, I can change shoes."

"Don't change a thing," he said, wondering if she was one of those women who, in the name of beauty, bought shoes that doubled as torture devices. "You're perfect."

She blushed, and it made something warm spread through his chest.

Denver. Little over a week.

He shoved aside his mixed feelings and focused instead on the reason for them. Not that she was the one giving him doubts. Not that he *had* doubts, but if he did, they wouldn't be coming from her. He had his sister and mother to blame for that. That Caitlin was the first woman to hold his attention in such a way meant nothing beyond the fact that he had a perpetual kickstand problem and no desire to take care of it without her.

"I'll take you at your word," she told him, "seeing as how you don't look ready to climb through the trees."

If only she knew what he would do right then. Anything, it seemed, but walking away, which was about the only way to get through his remaining time there unscathed. "Is that a challenge? Because I can always buy a new shirt."

Unscathed was overrated.

"It's definitely not a challenge, though I will say I'm curious what you have in mind."

Too bad she hadn't said that when he'd dropped her off after their lunch date. He hadn't even touched her for fear he'd want more, but who was he kidding? He *already* wanted more. And no sooner did he decide the hands-off approach was best than she showed up, asking for…a hand. One he'd been all too willing to give.

His resistance had held up for all of a minute.

Tonight promised less.

He opened the truck door for her, surprised when she didn't give him a hard time. She liked to do things herself—like pay for lunch—and he appreciated that, but it only made him want to do more for her.

Like what he'd planned for that night.

He fired up the truck, and ten minutes later, he steered into the lot of 34 West and Main. At twelve stories, the tower of granite and tinted glass wasn't the most impressive of so-called skyscrapers, but it was the tallest Dry Rock had to offer.

Caitlin peered through the windshield as he cut the engine. "What is this?"

"Mostly corporate office space." He hopped out and went around to open her door, not that she gave him much of a chance. She'd let herself out, though the entirety of her skirt had yet to fall from the seat, giving him a killer view of one smooth, creamy thigh. He imagined dragging his tongue along its length, then higher, and his mouth literally fucking watered.

She must have read his mind, because she smoothed the fabric, dislodging it from the seat, and looked around. "What are we doing here?"

She had no clue what he had in mind, and he loved that he had the chance to surprise her. "Tackling your fear of heights."

Skepticism reigned. "It was more the water under the bridge. I'm generally okay with office buildings."

"We'll see about that." He led her to the lobby, wishing the floors above were full of hotel suites instead of office space. Hell, even *one* suite. Anything to drive away this ache.

Or drive it home.

This section of town tended to clear out at the close of bank business, with foot traffic sparse. Most of it by that hour had moved toward the trendy, artsy district near the diner and the bookstore where the buildings were older, smaller, and boasted more of a nightlife. Though only a few blocks separated them, the difference was striking.

But Caitlin hadn't seen anything yet.

Shane led her to the front entrance, a wide swath of glass that gave him a startlingly normal view of the two of them, all couple-like. He shoved away the thought and punched a code into the keypad to let them in.

"Do you have an office here?" she asked, still sounding puzzled.

"No, but we do some after-hours training at this location." That was a whole other kind of ache. Maybe *that* was what he needed—a few hours of grueling physical exertion. He had focus when it counted.

Too bad it counted so damn much with her.

"You train in an office building?"

"The stairs." His legs ached and lungs burned just thinking about it. "We hit the stairwell in full turnout gear. Going up, you haul a hundred-pound fire hose. Coming down, you get to carry the dead weight of a one-hundred-and-eighty-pound dummy on your back and shoulders. And it's timed."

Caitlin looked impressed—something he doubted he'd

coaxed from her before that moment, but he'd love to see that look on her face again. Already, he was mentally calculating ways to impress her. Most of them involved nudity. "I doubt I could make it up more than two flights in leggings and trainers," she said. "Your department has nothing to fear from me."

"Until you find yourself on a bridge."

To her credit, she smiled. Forced or not, the way her face lit stunned him.

He turned his back on that and a dozen lascivious thoughts to lead her through the empty, dimly lit lobby to the elevator.

She hesitated a few feet away and stiffened when, after he hit the button, the door slid silently open, but the touch of his hand at the small of her back was enough to send her forward. He wondered about her hesitation. She couldn't possibly know what he had in mind. If she did, she wouldn't have held back on letting him know what she thought.

She winced when the doors shut.

Recognition hit. "Seriously?" he asked. "You can't be afraid of *everything*. Narrow it down a little."

She stared at him like he was an idiot. "I'm fine with spiders."

He tried not to let his shock show. He knew grown men who ran from spiders, though he wasn't one of them. He'd have put money on her being afraid of those. "And elevators?"

With a nervous glance around, she said, "There's not a building back in Wyatt with more than two floors. If you need to go up and you can walk, you take the stairs. But I'm a lot more worried about where we're headed than how we're getting there."

So maybe it wasn't so much fear as it was unfamiliarity. He pressed the button for the roof. It wasn't labeled with a thirteen, but it sat right after twelve. He bit back a grin when her eyes narrowed, though her words implied she'd suspected the top floor.

Just probably not what he *really* had in mind.

Just to keep the smile off his face, he asked, "Bridges, water, heights, fire…what else terrifies you? Let me guess—elevators."

"Not elevators," she said, glancing at the space. Mirrors made it seem bigger than it was, but they only occupied the top half. Beneath the rail, brushed stainless steel seemed to funnel toward the floor. "Not a fan of freefall, though."

The elevator jolted, and she gasped. He opened his mouth to give her a hard time, but the fear in her eyes was real.

Damn it. He hadn't meant to terrorize her with the elevator, of all things. She stood, frozen, and he realized that's what she'd been doing when he'd found her on the bridge. He wondered what was going on in her head. The direction of her gaze suggested she watched the numbers tick by. The elevator was slow, but horrifying seconds could feel like hours. He remembered that from losing his dad. Those words sitting there, lingering in air, waiting for someone to take them back. To call it a cruel joke, to say that his dad was soot-stained but otherwise okay, the smile he always wore fixed firmly in place.

Everyone had demons.

He just had a bad habit of running toward his.

She breathed an audible sigh of relief when the doors slid open, and so did he. He didn't need to be closed in with those memories. He didn't dwell. He moved forward.

So did Caitlin. She'd stepped out ahead of him and looked around, her eyes as wide as a child's. Not that he could blame her. This was one of his favorite places to have a drink, though it was far from a hotspot. In fact, the rooftop vestibule into which the elevator opened was long closed for the day. Still, the view couldn't be matched. Inside the glass-walled vista, bistro seating lined three-quarters of the perimeter, with a small café filling the rest. A smattering of tables filled the open space, but he knew it was the view beyond the glass that had grabbed her.

"What is this place?" Her voice was breathless, this time without a trace of fear.

"Think of it as a cafeteria," he said. "It was put here for the people who work in the building, but it's open to and seldom visited by the public." He likened it to a best-kept secret, and it was yet another place he'd never taken a date. Or whatever this was. Fortunately, he wouldn't be left to revisit this place without her. He'd find another rooftop somewhere, where the sunset had never set fire to her hair or bathed her face in that astounding light.

She walked over to the door and touched her fingertips to the glass, her eyes fixed on the world beyond. High above the trees, they had a clear view of the mountains to the west. In the foreground, a rooftop garden burst in a riot of summer blooms.

He reached past her to push open the door, and he didn't think he'd ever forget the excitement in her eyes when she turned to look at him in surprise. "We can go out there?"

"After you," he said. He loved the excitement in her voice, though it surprised him. Of course, they were in the center of a generously-sized patio, not hanging over the edge.

"I'm not getting on a ledge," she warned.

"I wouldn't let you if you tried." Which was true, but he couldn't shake the feeling that he'd ended up on one himself.

He followed her into the night air so thick with the scent of flowers drifting from planters of all shapes and sizes that he was surprised it didn't give him an instant headache. "Why is everyone in town not up here?" she asked. "It's beautiful."

"Well, for one, it's not open. Closes at three, and only open on weekdays. Otherwise, they probably prefer burgers and milkshakes."

"You think you're kidding," she said somberly, "but those were the two best milkshakes of my life."

So she'd remember him for something. Not that he cared. "I can't compete with that," he said, "but I do have some wine I'm told is good."

"You have wine?"

He found the insulated basket he'd left hidden before picking her up. "Wine and some glazed baked ham and Swiss rollup things."

She laughed. "Rollup things? Is that how you found them on a menu?"

"No, but I didn't memorize the menu, either. I just asked the chef what he recommended, and he threw this together for me." Shane had been in Dry Rock so long he knew pretty much everyone, including the man behind the menu at the best fine-dining establishment in town.

"A *chef* threw this together?" Was he imagining things, or had he actually managed to impress her? Her eyes sparkled. "And I thought we weren't dating."

"Who said we're dating?" The question was sincere, but something inside him protested over his protest. He'd dated, but he'd never done anything like this. Which meant it should count as a date. Either that, or it definitely didn't.

Neither option seemed right. Caitlin was different.

And she wasn't his. Never would be.

"It's already the best date of my life," she said. "It has to count as a date, or I'm going to have to admit to an embarrassingly mediocre dating history."

"That sounds like something I want to hear more about," he said, not bothering to share with her how closely his story mirrored hers. The last thing they needed was for him to admit they had something else in common. Instead, he poured two glasses of wine and took her hand, leading her toward the side. Early stars pierced the sky, and a cool mountain breeze stirred her hair against her nape. He wondered if it tickled. And what would happen if he kissed her there.

She hadn't mentioned the hand-holding, like that would be a conversation topic. But if there was a woman on the planet who would call him out for touching her, she was the one. She hadn't objected to their growing proximity to the side, either, so he kept moving.

By now, twilight had begun to settle on the mountains, giving them a purplish hue at the treetops that grew into a glowing ember reflecting on the barren rock and patches of snow higher up.

She had her attention pegged near her feet. He squeezed her hand, only for her to pull away. To his questioning look, she said, "I'm fine."

She didn't sound fine, but he let it go. "Check out that view." When she hesitated, he added, "There's absolutely no reason to look down. You can see everything straight ahead."

She did as he asked, then let out a long breath at the sight of the pink-and-purple streaked sky. "Wow."

Wow was right, though it didn't compare to the reflection in her eyes.

"This is the best not-a-date I've ever been on," she said. "Elevator and all."

So now they were back to the not-a-date thing. Only it was her best. He felt like a jerk for basking in the glory of that. And for wanting to be remembered…especially when he could only hope to forget her. He swallowed a spike of vulnerability when he realized how unlikely that was and tossed out the most generic response he could muster. "Then the guys you go out with need to step up their game."

She scoffed. "Because that's what every man wants to hear."

"You've got a point. I don't think I'd appreciate that very much."

"I figured that about you."

She hadn't taken her eyes off the view, so he couldn't get a read on her. Finally, he asked, "What's that supposed to mean?"

"You have women falling at your feet. Why would you listen to criticism when you can just move on to someone who tells you what you want to hear?"

Her words hit home. She wasn't wrong, though he'd never thought of it that way. Which as far as he was concerned meant he wasn't that kind of guy. "Who says I have women falling at my feet?"

"Am I wrong?"

"I'm pretty sure no one has actually fallen." He realized the unexpected truth behind the words after he said them aloud. He'd never felt the kind of connection he'd even begin to call love, and as far as he could tell, he'd never devastated a woman by ending things. Most of the time, they stayed friends, or at least friendly, so he wasn't losing much. Missing intimacy, he now realized, but he'd never had it walk away from him. He'd just never really had it at all.

"A literal response and an attempt at deflection. Nice."

He met her eyes. "Criticize me, since you think I can't take it."

"And be left on the roof?"

"You have my word I will not leave you up here, toss or push or otherwise fling you off the side, or request a helicopter to airlift you out of here. So here's your chance. Tell me what I'm doing wrong."

After a moment, she spoke. "Well, first of all, you told me about the food and didn't let me have any."

Relief surged. "Let me fix that right now." He left her long enough to grab the cooler and its contents, then brought it back to the nearest table. The ham roll wrap things were in a foil container with a clear plastic lid—not the prettiest presentation, but this wasn't a date. He handed her one with a napkin and cracked open a bottle of iced water for himself.

"Second," she said, "you keep giving me phallic-shaped food."

He choked and nearly spit the water. *Oh shit,* he did. "Unintentional. I swear."

"Third—"

He stared. "There are three things? Really?"

"*Third*, you insist on torturing me with things that terrify me."

"Wait a minute," he protested. "You requested this one. You said, and I quote, *I want to tackle my fear of heights*."

"Fourth," she said with a grin, "despite that, and the fact that we are not dating, this is still one of the three best dates of my life."

"Really, that's a criticism?" He paused. "What were the other ones?"

"Things you and I did together. And I don't want to hear it, so just don't. Your ego has been stroked enough."

Stroked. Shit. He was quiet for a moment before he said, "So I bring the phallic objects and you discuss stroking things? Is that where we are?"

She laughed, but then sobered. "Rumor has it we're headed in two different directions, which precludes any chance of there being a *we* to locate. That might be different under different circumstances, but under different circumstances, we wouldn't be here."

"I guess it's a good thing, then," he lied, swallowing that unwelcomed bit of reality with another shot of water. "And we're not done here."

"We aren't? Because I have to tell you, I'm not getting any closer to the edge."

Good for her, because he couldn't seem to take a step back to save his life. He took the glass from her and set it aside. "What I meant," he said, "is that it's my turn to criticize."

"I don't think I agreed to that."

"You're stubborn," he said anyway. "And a drain on civic resources."

"Well, I've heard one of those before," she grumbled.

He touched her cheek, causing her to meet his gaze with wide eyes. "And you're beautiful."

"Flattering, but generic."

"The color of your eyes, it's like walking through the woods in the spring." Would he ever do that again and not see her?

"Less generic," she murmured.

He toyed with the ever-present chaos of her hair where it escaped its knot. "And this. I don't even know how hair can seem so cheerful, but I see it sticking out and it makes me smile."

"A little strange," she said.

"Do you trust me?" he asked.

"Yes," she whispered, guarded, but she'd said it.

He let go of her and walked to the edge, leaning against the thigh-high concrete barrier with his back to the drop. There was still a ledge below, so he wasn't risking much, but she didn't know that. "Come here."

She gave him the most convincing *oh hell no* expression he'd ever seen in his life. "Not even if you had a gallon of wine and an actual phallus."

"I've got news for you sweetheart. I've got both. Now come here."

She rolled her eyes, but the indifference of the gesture didn't disguise her fear.

"I'm not coming after you," he told her. "You need to make this decision on your own. It's why we're up here, right?"

She edged away from him, toward the insulated bag. "I'm going to need more of that wine."

"Nope. The wine isn't going to do it, either. This needs to be you."

She sighed—annoyed, he hoped—and took a step toward him. Then one more, half the length of the first. The third was more of a wobble.

"The staff will be here by three a.m.," he said, doing his best to sound bored.

Shot him a glare. Another small step accompanied it. "At what point," she asked, eyeing the distance between them, "can I call it close enough?"

"When you're as close to me now as you were on the bike."

Not even the heavy dusk could hide her blush. "I find that highly unnecessary."

"There's a fifty-six story building in Denver. If we have to do this there instead…" Damned if he couldn't see that. He *wanted* it.

"I don't recall telling you I'd get anywhere near Denver."

He'd been joking, but her refusal to visit dinged his pride. At least one of them had some sense. "Come. Here," he said.

She took a shaky breath and hitched her gaze to his. "Okay, I'm going to be straight with you. If I get any closer, I'm not going to be able to breathe. It'll be the bridge all over again."

"Trust me. I've got you."

She shook her head. "I've never trusted anyone that much."

He took a step toward her and leaned to whisper in her ear. "Start."

Then he retreated.

She grimaced. Tears touched her eyes, but she held his gaze and closed the distance, one painful step at a time. He couldn't imagine living with such fear, but he could see in her eyes it was real. And he'd do anything to take it from her.

"Just look at me," he said. "And let me tell you about me."

"You?" One word, and yet her voice wavered.

"Yep. All about me."

"If you're going to detail your dating situation…" she said faintly, dragging him back to the moment they'd met. It felt like a year ago, and she'd so thoroughly consumed his thoughts since then that he honestly couldn't remember a single moment before it. At least not without inserting thoughts of her.

"You're safe from that." He wiped an escaped tear off her cheek. "So, stuff about me. I'm not an adrenaline junkie—"

"Says Lieutenant Must-go-somewhere-more-exciting."

He ignored the jab, despite the laser-precision delivery. Mainly so he wouldn't have to tell her how much better she made the mundane stuff. Like this rooftop. He'd seen it a hundred times, but even when he'd hit it after a twelve-story run, his heart hadn't skipped like this. "As I was saying, I'm not all about the thrill. But there's this feeling up here. I don't know if it's the mountain or the air or the feeling of freedom, but it comes from being on the edge."

She scowled. "Um, isn't that the definition of an adrenaline junkie?"

"I like the feeling of being up here. Not of falling off."

"Didn't you tell me you'd jumped out of a plane? Twice?"

Jesus, this woman. "Caitlin, I swear to God."

She smiled sweetly, though it was strained.

So they were doing this *again*, but the fear was gone. He'd take it. He tugged her closer, and she whimpered a soft protest. She landed against him, standing between his parted legs. The combination of her high heels and his leaning against the ledge left them on even ground, height-wise.

Her eyes grew wide with alarm. Or maybe it was the same fear he felt, growing and churning and having nothing to do with the distance between his feet and the earth several floors below.

"It's like having a beautiful woman in your arms," he said, ignoring a veritable explosion of second thoughts, to say nothing of whatever she must be thinking. Whatever it was didn't matter. He had her, and he had no intention of letting go. "Thinking you want to kiss her. Not really wanting her to push you off a roof."

"Is that your abstract analogy?"

"It's not entirely abstract," he admitted.

Caitlin pursed her lips, then softly said, "She doesn't *completely* want to push you off the roof."

It was a good thing he was half sitting, or he'd have fallen over. "Damn good thing," he whispered, right before he dipped his head and kissed her. He hadn't intended to take it too far, but when she softened against him, he was screwed. Fingers threading her hair, hand cupping the back of her head, drawing her in, needing her for his next breath *screwed*.

What the *fuck*.

He should have seen it coming from a mile away. He hadn't been able to shake the first kiss, despite his attempts to convince himself it was a fluke. Hell, first kisses were *supposed* to be memorable.

Second kisses weren't supposed obliterate them. And they weren't supposed to make him wonder why he'd ever stop kissing her to go to Denver.

Panicking, he broke it off, just barely aware of the awkward timing of having just deepened the kiss before abandoning it.

Caitlin stared at him, flushed. Sexy. Her lips were swollen, her glasses askew. He felt like hell over it, but he needed to get out of there. Keeping her off-balance was one thing. Losing his own equilibrium was another.

"We should probably go back downstairs," he finally said. "If I'm going to accidentally trigger an alarm and drag a security guard back out here, it'd better be before he gets in bed."

"Oh," she said. The hurt in her eyes felt like splinters gouging at raw skin, but he needed the ground under his feet.

Just not at her expense. "You did it, you know."

He'd have given anything for criticism number five right then, but she didn't throw any jabs.

She didn't say anything at all.

He felt bad, but she'd scared the hell out of him. His desire to fall into her was scarier than any twelve-story drop could ever be, and he hadn't meant to do it, but he'd hurt her.

And he had no idea what to do about his fucked-up desire to fix something that needed to stay broken.

Chapter Thirteen

Caitlin had to give Shane all the credit in the world. She'd completely forgotten about the hundred and twenty-ish feet that stood between her and solid ground, or how much of a bad idea he was. And that he was leaving.

She'd never been kissed like that. Not at her front door, and certainly not on a roof.

Nor had she ever run a guy off so quickly.

One minute she was about to melt right into the rooftop, and the next, the air had gone cold without him. He'd gone from soft touch and a kiss that was as gentle as it was lethal to throwing stuff back in the basket and heading for the elevator, sparing only one backward glance to make sure she followed.

She managed to keep her mouth shut until the elevator door slid closed, until panic began to well and any distraction was better than none at all.

"Did I stab you in the eye with my glasses or something?"

He glanced at her, muttered something that sounded an awful lot like *fuck*, and smacked his hand against the emergency stop button.

The elevator lurched to a standstill.

She clutched the railing that lined the wall. "This is *not* funny."

"You're goddamn right it's not," he said. "You've crossed a bridge, stood on top of the tallest building in Dry Rock, and you've ridden in an elevator. Twice. But this thing between us? We're both dodging it."

"I'm not the one who walked away up there," she said. But hadn't she been relieved when he had? He was as good as gone, and she couldn't seem to grasp that. The last thing she needed was to drown in this man.

Or maybe that was exactly what she did need.

He stood still, watching her, completely unfettered that she'd called him out for walking away. But he'd stopped the elevator.

Let him walk now.

She took a shaky step—damn her inability to do that without quaking—and grabbed him, hauling him down and claiming his mouth with hers.

He hesitated for the barest of seconds before muttering an oath with her name behind it and diving in. Hot, hard, against the wall, driving deep whatever they'd just dodged on the roof.

When they came up for air, she feared it was over, but he touched her again, gently this time, but no less thorough. She'd always heard of drowning in kisses, but had never imagined how adequate the description. The space between them was hot, stormy, his teeth nipping, his tongue coaxing shivers and lust from every corner of her body. The wall at her back couldn't have been harder than the man who'd captured her.

The sweetness of the wine lingered, but it wasn't what dizzied her. Clutching his hair, feeling his groan rumble through her, the moment he lifted and held her against the wall…yeah, heights had nothing on that. She'd *kill* for heights like this.

If she'd known this could happen in an elevator, she'd have lived in one of the damned things.

Shane abandoned her mouth long enough to kiss her neck and murmur into her ear, "I'll stop if you want me to."

"I don't want you to stop," she told him, her voice trembling with every slam of her heart against her chest. "But this isn't my typical protocol for a first date."

He looked to her breast, where he traced her straining nipple through her dress, then back at her face.

She'd never seen so much in one expression. So much… not holding back. Like she'd just unleashed something, and every part of her begged to be swept away with it.

And she'd never felt so much as she did when his gaze tripped over hers and the moment lingered, on the cusp of something big, before he spoke so softly, lips grazing the corner of her mouth when he said, "Then it's a damn good thing this isn't a date, isn't it?"

• • •

Shane had never ached like this. His balls were probably bluer than the depths of the Pacific, and that was despite her telling him to keep going. It didn't make sense. He was hardly deprived, but he wanted this woman like he'd never wanted anyone.

And her green-lighting him only made him want her more.

There went the theory of the chase.

He couldn't get enough of her mouth. He coveted that damned thing, despite its insistence of throwing insults and giving him a hard time. He devoured her, sweet and soft, tasting the hunger, throbbing, *needing*. Her kisses met his, tentative when he pulled back, consuming when he let go.

He lifted her away from the wall long enough to slide his hands along the bare skin of her legs, past her hips, higher. Hot skin on hot skin, he swore he felt her heat through his pants.

He *hurt*.

His dick clamored to be set free, but he kept it in his pants. If he didn't, he was going to end up balls deep, shaking the car until even *he* thought it might take a multi-story plunge. And really, he'd rather be able to take his time, to worship his way through every slick part and fold.

She was going to kill him.

"Tell me to stop," he practically begged. It was the only chance he had of saving himself. But she dug her nails against his skull as he bit down on her breast through the dress. He wanted the garment gone, nothing between them but heat, but he couldn't just fuck her in an *elevator*.

"No."

Her simple reply undid him, though a touch of his own incredulity edged through the haze of sexual inebriation. "You're actually refusing to cooperate with stopping me?" he managed.

"You started the fire, Lieutenant," she said, all breathy and sexy. "I'm pretty sure it's your civic duty to put it out."

Put it out, hell. This was starting something. Something he wasn't sure he could handle, but if he was going down, he was going down hard.

Literally.

He let her go again, which earned an expression of near fury until he yanked the dress over her head.

"You're lucky there wasn't a zipper," she gasped, which was as close to a grudging admission that he'd had a good idea as he'd ever get from her. "I could have died."

"I looked ahead of time," he told her, right before he unhooked her bra and dropped his head to one hard nipple.

"Oh God," she moaned, throwing back her head. "Oh *God*. There's a camera in here, isn't there."

"Where?" He didn't actually care, but he knew he should. He didn't need the footage getting back to the chief or anyone else he knew.

"In the corner. It's camera shaped."

He laughed at her blunt description, then tossed her bra over the lens. "Better?" Without waiting for an answer, he dropped to his knees and with one hand on each hip, inched down her panties.

"Why am I the only one without clothes?"

"We're addressing your fears, not mine." He spread her center with his thumbs and wasted approximately zero seconds in thought before sucking her into his mouth. No foreplay there. Straight to the clit.

Her grip tightened like a snapped rubber band, leaving him utterly convinced she'd ripped out hair by the handful.

He didn't care.

He rasped his tongue across the swollen bud, relenting only to drive deep inside her while she squirmed against him. He listened to the sounds she made, taking notes, switching gears between sucking and licking, plunging and biting, keeping her from catching her breath, hiding his own dizziness.

He widened her stance, trying to spread her legs farther, but she'd only managed to kick off one leg of her underwear. Easy enough to fix. He slid a pair of fingers inside, curving them until he found the spot that made her knees buckle. The way she breathed his name made him want to hear it across crisp sheets, elevator be damned, but he wouldn't trade this now, her legs opened wide for him, sounds of wanting him on her lips. He found her clit with his tongue, then captured the swollen bundle of nerves with his teeth while the naughty librarian uttered words that would make a sailor blush.

So she had a wild side.

Good. To. Know.

She trembled in his hands, on his mouth, undeniably close to an edge.

He licked long and hard.

She climbed the wall behind her, pulling him in for the ride. He didn't relent, probably couldn't if he tried, with the grip she'd managed despite his short hair, but wouldn't have missed it for anything. The look in her eyes when they focused unsteadily on his left him shaken, not necessarily in a good way. It was a way that shouldn't happen between people moving so quickly in different directions, but he coveted the intense haze of the connection.

He didn't know how he'd ever forget it.

He didn't know that he'd want to.

And he didn't want her to, either. Fingertips teasing her inner thighs, his mouth alive with the taste of her, he drove his tongue deeper, sucking and barely holding on when she shattered and damn near took him down with her.

Her body shook. He let her slide down the wall to land on his lap. Agony. He dragged his tongue across her nipple, loving the fullness. The fucking intimacy. When she jerked in surprise, he bit down. She touched the back of his head, forcing him closer, and he wondered if she was still coming down or if he was on the verge of riling her again. Even from his vantage point, it had been a hell of ride—one his dick would never forgive him for sitting out.

Regret edged over common sense and decency, blowing it out of the water when she moaned and arched against him. "You have no idea how good that feels," she said in a low, sexy voice. Her glasses were almost sideways, so he nudged them back in place and licked the other nipple.

She glanced down. "We totally left you hanging, didn't we?"

He groaned. "I can assure you, there's no hanging."

She reached for his zipper. "Not fair to you."

He placed a hand on her arm. "Sweetheart, I want you more than you can imagine, but I need this to be about you." He didn't need to forge more of a connection than he already felt, and while he was content for her to associate elevators with sex, he'd do well to spare himself a similar connotation.

"So this is where it ends? I'm naked in an elevator and you're not even missing a button?"

"You have shoes," he managed, adjusting himself when she moved off of him to grab her clothes. "Not naked."

She shot him a dirty look, then reached for her bra and missed. She jumped for it the second time and caught the edge, flinging it toward the ceiling before it fell.

He couldn't help but smile. God, she was beautiful. He entertained second thoughts about where he'd have her, and suddenly against the wall of an elevator was right at the top of his list.

But he didn't get the chance to reconsider, because she chose this of all times not to argue. Instead, she stuffed her underwear in her bag and pulled the dress over her head, leaving him all too aware of what was—or rather, was *not*—under the fabric.

And wanting.

Wanting something Denver couldn't possibly offer.

He'd yet to draw to his feet, and she'd already hit the button, sending the elevator back into motion. "We're going to have to make a stop on the way back to my place," she said.

"For what?"

"A way to help me live with that memory once you're gone," she said, and not a word more until the door slid open on the ground floor, when she literally stepped over him to leave the elevator, wine bottle in hand.

He sat there way too long, wondering how the fuck he was supposed to do that, when she threw an addendum his way.

"I'm going to need some batteries."

Chapter Fourteen

So much for being afraid of heights.

Caitlin was about a million miles above earth, her old grounded self a mere pinprick in the distance.

Dizzy was an understatement.

Breathing into a paper bag seemed like a plan right about then.

But there was no paper bag. There was Shane, a stalled-out elevator, and the best orgasm of her life zinging through her body like he'd tied her up with a live wire and teased her to delicious agony.

If the memory of that night was going to have to sustain her, she'd need a whole crate of batteries.

Refilled monthly.

She didn't think he'd actually heed her request, so when he steered into a drug store parking lot she had to fight the urge to crawl under the floor mat. "Um, thank you, but I'm not going to put my underwear on in a parking lot to go in there."

"You're not going to have to," he said, right before he

hopped out of the truck, a bit less agile than usual. That last part left her with a smile, but also teeming with guilt. She should have insisted on taking care of him, but the sincerity in his eyes when he said he wanted it to be about her had stopped her.

He returned within minutes and tossed what had to be a twenty-pound bag on the seat between them. "I'm just going to tell myself the need for these isn't due to a lack of satisfaction on your part," he muttered as he adjusted himself.

She gawked at his lap, then flushed hot when she realized he watched her. "How many…battery operated devices do you think I own?"

"To be honest, I'm not sure I would have guessed any, at least not before I knew you were running a sex library." He threw her a cocky grin while she died inside. "To answer the question I think you're asking, you didn't specify what kind you needed."

She dug through the bag and pulled out a card. "Shane, these are hearing aid batteries."

He clicked his seatbelt in place and backed out of the spot. "Do I look like I know what kind of batteries a vibrator takes?"

She held up another package. "Do I look like someone who would go through *thirty-six* double AAs?"

"Have you ever checked the unit price on those things? Much cheaper to get the bigger packs."

Speechless, she leaned back against the seat and ticked off a list of what she'd just learned about him: he paid attention to unit prices and bought name brand batteries. And no condoms, which meant—contrary to the accusation she'd levied earlier—he hadn't made any assumptions on the rest of the night.

She wished she could appreciate that more.

Back at her house, he walked her to the door. Light from

the porch fixture threw shadows, darkening a hint of stubble on his jaw. It would be gone with his next shift, she was sure, but in the meantime, the hint of badassery made her knees weak.

He hesitated.

She stood without even digging for her keys, because she had no idea what would come next. Should she invite him in? Was he hoping she wouldn't? He had just given her a year's supply of batteries…well, other than the Cs. And he hadn't bought any condoms, so surely he wasn't planning anything. But if that was the case, why wasn't he going away?

"What are you thinking so hard about?" he asked, breaking the long silence with something way worse.

She didn't need to confess to wanting him. Heat tore through her, turning her into a neon-pink billboard of *want*. Anxiety left her chewing on her lip and quite possibly breaking a sweat.

Sexy.

She pushed up her glasses, then wondered why she had any desire to see better. A cock-eyed version of the world was probably preferable. Only that poor word choice hadn't helped.

Her gaze crept to his. With any luck he'd think her ridiculous and flee. She could go on about her life, trying like crazy not to get stuck on any bridges or start any fires on his shift until what was left of those two weeks were up. Then life would be normal.

Like normal existed after she'd had an elevator orgasm thanks to a man whose talents in setting fires *had* to rival his ability to put them out.

Leave it to her to freeze on a bridge in front of a sexual pyromaniac.

"I'm not. Thinking, that is." She sputtered the words.

They were laughably true.

She didn't have a chance to laugh, though, because he did, and before she could ask him what was so funny his mouth was on hers. And so was the rest of him. He was a force, but the kiss was soft. So incredibly soft. She sighed against his mouth, then erupted with a tiny shriek when he hoisted her against the door. Self-preservation caused her to tighten her thighs against his waist, her legs hooking around his back.

Under a porch light.

For the entire neighborhood to see.

His mouth closed on her earlobe.

Oh hell. Let them look. If Shane kept kissing her like this, her days were numbered anyway.

"Where are your keys?" He murmured the words, his lips grazing her ear, his teeth punctuating with a promised ferocity that belied the benign, if utterly loaded, question.

"Keys?" Her glasses had gone awry. She blinked, dazed, but he didn't come into focus.

"Either we get that door open, or the neighbors are *really* going to have something to talk about."

"Oh." It was the lamest *oh* in existence. "In my..." She fumbled for her bag, which flapped at her side as she tried to grasp it. "Somewhere."

"May I?" he asked.

She nodded, and within seconds he had her keys in his hand. There were only two on the chain—the old bookstore key and the brand new one for her house—and he made quick work of figuring out which was which, sending the door flying inward on the heels of his success. She expected she'd fall in after it, but he had her.

As if to cement that, in one swift move he'd kicked the door shut. He fumbled at her back, and the *snick* of the lock somehow made itself heard over the sounds of their traded breaths. He sat her on the back of her loveseat and slid his hands up her body, setting fire to her skin. Cool air touched her heated flesh, and she realized she was five seconds from being the only naked person in the room.

Again.

Hell no.

This was crazy, and she didn't do crazy.

At least, she didn't do crazy *alone*.

Before he could get her arms over her head, she countered by yanking at his shirt, sending buttons pinging. She opened two stragglers with more traditional methods then tugged the shirt off his arms. The sight of him shirtless, his body doused in ambient light, muscles defined by shadow, left her throbbing. Why couldn't her body forget that orgasm?

Why would she *want* it to?

He'd been all about getting her out of her clothes, but when she'd turned the tables on him, he'd stilled. Her gaze dropped from the bone-melting intensity of those dark eyes to the trail of hair leading below the belt, and she went there, too. With shaking hands, she worked at the button then eased down the zipper.

Then she reached inside.

"Caitlin." He managed her name, then a few choice words when he sprung free and she immediately dropped to her knees and took him in her mouth. "Oh shit."

She had no idea a single profane word could be so erotic. Actually, pre-elevator, she wasn't exactly familiar with truly erotic situations. Tolerable, better than nothing, she could live with herself in the morning, maybe got close to an orgasm, yes. Completely forgetting for any number of seconds that she was in public had not happened. Ever. She'd never truly believed it could.

And dropping to her knees in front of a guy…well, that wasn't exactly something she did. And a man who expected otherwise would be better off protecting himself than exposing himself, but Shane wasn't going to get her naked twice. Not without joining her.

Somehow she doubted he'd chalk this up to a loss.

She glanced up, slightly self-conscious, and found his head tipped back toward the ceiling and one hand planted against the wall that stood a couple of feet behind him. His entire ridiculously sculpted torso was tense, the muscles sharply defined by the play of shadow. One hand rested against the back of her head, and she couldn't believe how gentle that touch was with his arm so tight with tension.

She'd take that as a compliment.

Go, her.

Taking him deeper was more of a struggle than she cared to admit, not just because of his size, but because her skills weren't exactly on point. But what little she could see of him from her knees suggested she didn't suck. Or maybe she did, and that was the point, but either way, she settled for sliding her tongue along his length, engulfing him, then drawing him deeper. What started as a personal challenge not to be one-upped had heat pooling, and in a flash, fire raging. She had elevator flashbacks, back to that orgasm from which her limbs had yet to recover, and all those doubts faded and she suddenly felt empowered. He'd been hard when she'd taken him in her mouth. Now he was granite, even larger, and unless she'd just lost track of gravity, he trembled.

All because of what she was doing to him.

She took him deeper, rising higher on her knees to change the angle, feeling like hot shit while he cursed and hissed. Then the gentle touch faded. He grabbed her hair and held her back, his arm tight with tension.

She looked up, blinking innocently. Feeling anything but.

He drew deep breaths but said nothing, and his hold on her hair kept her from diving back in, but she did manage to stick out her tongue far enough to lick the swollen head.

"*Fuck*." He let go of her, gently deflecting her next move, and closed his hand on himself, a groan slipping from his lips.

Well, then. She adjusted her glasses and decided there was a definite downside to not letting things get too far…this slightly awkward moment blew all the others out of the water. She'd always heard there wasn't any such thing as a bad blow job, yet he'd just stopped her.

She wasn't sure whether she should be mortified or kick him out.

"Caitlin."

She met his gaze, expecting pity.

She got danger. Fire.

"I'm taking you to bed."

"Okay?"

"You might want to tell me where to look for a bed," he warned, "because if you don't I'm going to knock down every goddamn door in this place until I find one."

• • •

Shane couldn't breathe. Jesus fucking Christ, that woman. Not his first blow job. Not by a long shot. But she'd spared him the suction, instead licking, flicking her tongue around so one minute there was abrasion and the next nothing but slick, wet heat. Nothing to brace himself against. Just…fuck. That damnable woman with the clunky glasses and librarian act looking up at him with his dick in her mouth was every fantasy he hadn't known he had. She hadn't needed to swallow every inch. Or even half of them. Whatever she'd done was pure fucking magic, and he wasn't ready for it to be over.

His balls screamed in protest. His dick throbbed. No amount of logical argument from that threadbare connection he still had with his brain felt like enough. The only thing that kept him from exploding was the thought of breaking that spell…of having the world's most effective overthinker lump him into bridge and elevator territory and back away, right back to that place she'd retreated where she'd gotten all shy after he'd done some licking and sucking of his own.

But no way that compared to this.

"End of the hall," she told him, her tone a bit timid.

Yeah, well, if she had any clue what he had on his mind, it damn well ought to be.

He scooped her up and tossed her over his shoulder, giving life to every caveman accusation she'd ever levied his way, and headed off in the direction she'd indicated. The short hallway seemed a hundred miles long, and what he found at the end shouldn't have surprised him. The room was immaculate, the bed made, pillows neatly placed, corners tight.

All of it about to go to hell.

He tossed her on the bed and didn't give her time to catch her breath before he dragged the dress over her head, leaving it caught on her arms. There wasn't a bra in his way this time, and before she'd managed a full breath he closed his mouth on her tight nipple, causing her back to bow and her breath to hiss. He took full advantage, sliding his arm beneath her, moving her up the bed, crawling after her. The pillows scattered, and his pants snagged on the side of the bed, dragging to his ankles. He kicked them off, never releasing the suction on her breast.

Her nails, short as they were, tore through his hair without gaining purchase. She must have given up, because the pressure relented and then she was fisting the comforter, arching against him with the dress still caught on her wrists.

He ached. God, he fucking ached. But he ignored that, dipping his head from one greedy nipple to the next, the tight buds begging for the heat of his tongue. When he didn't think he could stand it a moment longer, he abandoned them both, dragging his tongue to the valley between her breasts, licking playfully, trying like hell not to ruin her pretty flowered quilt with his growing need to lose control.

She shivered and panted, and the dress he hadn't fully removed was in his goddamned way. He tugged at it, just about to untangle her when an opportunity presented itself. She wanted to stay dressed?

She'd rather take his dick in that hot little mouth, skew her glasses, and bat those innocent wide eyes at him?

Yeah, he'd play like that.

Gently, he moved her arms over her head. She blinked accusatorily at him, but he distracted her by nipping at her breast, then sucking her fingers into his mouth when he couldn't maneuver her hands the way he wanted from that angle.

Her eyes widened, then drifted closed, leaving him to do a sloppy job of twisting the fabric, tangling it so her hands were caught by the headboard. Hell. Not what he'd wanted, but she'd have a hard time getting them free to return his touch, which meant he might last five minutes.

He returned his attention to her breasts, grazing one, then the other, then kissing his way to her side, licking warmth back into the tiny shivers that pebbled her skin. She wriggled and groaned when he spread her legs, then made a sound of utter frustration when he traced his tongue in the crease between her leg and her center. He loved that she tried to maneuver him toward the middle, and her lingering flavor made him want to go there so badly, but he wasn't going to give in just yet. Not when he was on the verge of exploding, and especially not when he had this obstinate woman begging for release. She didn't have to say it aloud. He could see it, with her lip caught in her mouth and her glasses askew and her punishing grip on the twisted and probably ruined dress, hips lifting until he could taste her without dipping his head.

Damned if he hadn't gotten so distracted by how beautiful she was that he'd temporarily abandoned his determination to tease the ever-loving fuck out of her.

"*Please*." The breathless word seemed as much caught in agony as it was pleasure. He responded by inserting a single finger, to which she managed to gasp, "funny."

Yeah, it was. He curled the digit inside her, finding that spot that made her shake, and toyed with it, lazily, while she shuddered and possibly cursed at him.

The proper librarian definitely had a naughty side—one that extended well beyond words.

His balls were about to explode.

"Don't move," he told her, momentarily abandoning her to search the floor for his jeans and the condom he kept in his wallet. Cliché as fuck, but she didn't have to know he'd put it there just for her. What he'd thought had been blind hope had turned into a woeful understatement, because he had a feeling they could go through an entire box and he'd still want her. But he hadn't bought any, because she'd lay him out in a heartbeat over that shit. And not in the good way.

He found the package and snagged it, then tossed his wallet on the floor. Just rolling it on almost finished him, and he didn't want to think of how pathetic that was, but it wasn't every day he had her waiting for him.

Still, he paused at her entrance, giving her one last chance to stop this thing from happening.

Someone had to save him from this need tearing through him.

But it wasn't going to be her.

She just spread her legs wider.

"Fuck." He eased inside her then, using all the restraint he could summon to make sure she was ready before he did any real damage. And she was. She was tight, slick, and pulsing. Hot. His arms shook with restraint to not thrust hard, take it all, feel everything.

She tugged at the tangled dress while she throbbed around

his dick, squeezing and torturing him. It was all he could do to keep his shit together. One condom was a mistake.

Fully seated, balls deep, feeling things from her body he'd never felt before in his life, he was hit yet another something to grapple with: she'd wrangled her arms free from the headboard and wrapped them around his neck, her sloppily tied hands managing to find his head, her fingertips curling against his scalp, and kissed him.

He'd never been deeper in a woman in his life. He'd never been kissed like that, ever. Not even by her, because she'd traded that tentative first touch for something that felt sure, for once like she didn't need to ask permission to slide her tongue against his. She just did it, deep and sweet, until he wasn't sure what was her and what was him.

It didn't feel like fucking.

It felt like owning.

He didn't break the kiss. Wouldn't for anything. And maybe he should give her more credit, because he couldn't slam into her that way. He could only rock softly, never really leaving the warmth of her body, while he sucked on her tongue and nipped at her mouth and let her utterly destroy him.

God, he was fucked.

The pressure built, like he was doing things his way, driving her into next week with the power of his thrusts. But he wasn't. He was lost to this shit, this gentle grind that dizzied him like nothing ever had, and he couldn't help but wonder if she somehow did this on purpose, keeping him off-balance like she had. Turning his game against him, trapping him with wrists that couldn't possibly still be bound, holding him tighter, deeper, her teeth nipping at him while her body took everything until he couldn't take it anymore.

He broke the kiss, or whatever that was that had him lost to her mouth, and twisted her hips so he straddled one leg and held the other, scissors-style, and ground against her clit until she definitely, without a doubt, said something profane.

He didn't relent.

He pushed as deep as he could without fear of hurting her, only to have her claw at his skin and demand more. She didn't have to ask twice. He pumped harder, thicker, slamming the headboard against the wall, giving only a passing thought to whether there might be any open windows or noise reaching the neighbors.

He held out until her body shuddered, giving the same treatment to his dick as it had his tongue, and then came harder than he ever had in his life. He lost his fucking eyesight for a good thirty seconds, long enough to wonder what the hell, before sparkles fought their way back from the periphery, leading to a fuzzy vision of her in his arms. For a moment he wondered if he'd just had the best dream of his life, until she stroked his cheek and said something about liking the stubble and how now he'd gone and ruined vibrators and probably her life. It all came through on a buzz, fading without fanfare, until he gave up and eased out of her, grateful and surprised to see the condom still intact.

No way he'd be able to get up yet to get rid of that thing. But he would. And ten more if she'd let him.

Until then, he dragged her close and tried like hell not to think about Denver.

Chapter Fifteen

Waking so utterly *not* alone probably should have startled the hell out of Caitlin, but despite sleeping like a rock, the connection to Shane was so there that she didn't do that sleepy morning-after double take requisite in so many of her favorite romance novels. She just felt…content. Which didn't sound like the most exciting thing in the world, but it beat the anxiety that normally clawed its way into her morning-afters.

Especially when the guy in question was still very much there.

And God, his eyelashes. She spent way too long staring at them, hating him for their length.

The man was astutely gifted with the length of a lot of things, it seemed.

He was also still asleep, but not likely to stay that way with her gawking. People could feel that kind of attention in their sleep, couldn't they? Back in high school, she'd wake on weekend mornings to find her cat staring at her, so stare-rousing had to be a thing.

It shouldn't be a thing when she still had morning breath.

She hit the shower, the water like needles against her skin. Was there any part of her he hadn't touched? And why the heck was she so willing to wash that off?

Because he's leaving.

It didn't matter how right he felt. It didn't matter where this thing could go, because it couldn't.

She was 100 percent sure she didn't want a long-distance relationship. Maybe if they had a history that required more than one calendar page, or if there was anything temporary about their different directions. But she wasn't going anywhere, and he wasn't coming back. There was no compromise in that.

All of this was for the better. She didn't need to second-guess the reason she felt better waking wound in his arms than she ever had alone. She didn't need to worry about losing him to some needy, bubbly, D-cup woman wearing size two skinny jeans. Caitlin thought herself far more awesome than that, but guys rarely did. Call her jaded, but she didn't need to wait for that moment.

She needed to get rid of the fire-fighting, bridge-slaying lieutenant in her bed.

But he'd gotten rid of himself.

When she left the bathroom, she found her bed empty. And made. Even the pillows were back where she kept them. Impressive, considering there'd only been a couple of seconds of observation time—in the dark, no less—before they'd skewed everything. Heat and electricity hit her, her body woefully, wonderfully sore and not the least bit chill with its recent state of being wholly, completely, devastatingly ravaged.

And then there was that tantalizing smell coming from the kitchen.

She gave herself a quick once-over with her barely discernible makeup routine and found Shane in the kitchen, frying bacon.

Shirtless.

"I'm pretty sure you're not supposed to do that," she said.

He gave a playful grin. "Fry bacon? Please tell me you don't eat it raw."

Must he be such a pain? "No one eats it raw. It's supposed to be—"

He held out a piece. "Just crispy enough to be crispy. No burnt flavor."

She took the bacon and popped it in her mouth. Her eyes closed in what had to look like exaggerated pleasure, but it wasn't. Not one bit. "You put this on your Tinder profile," she said, "and you'll have women beating down your door."

"How does one word that?" He feigned thought. "Once you put my meat in your mouth you're going to want to swallow?"

Her eyes widened before she could reel in the reaction. She swallowed, then flushed hotly over the fact that she'd done precisely what he'd predicted. Which was stupid, because what sane person didn't want to swallow bacon? "Probably won't get you the classiest of dates."

"But does it attract hot librarians?"

If he didn't stop calling her a librarian, she was going to… nothing. He was leaving. That problem would solve itself. "You'd have to find one to ask her."

"You. Quit being modest." His light, teasing tone was gone, and she wanted to tell him to stop being serious, or pretending to be, because all of the sudden she was caught up in that post-sex freak-out guys absolutely dreaded, or so she'd heard, because *never* had she been there, where she needed distance.

Now, not next week. She didn't want to think about how far she'd fall in a week.

But she said none of that, instead just hitting him with yet another reminder. "I'm a bookstore owner, not a librarian."

"And I'm not on Tinder or any other dating apps. I troll bridges."

"You got the troll part right," she said under her breath. *Distance*.

He flashed a crooked grin, then handed her another piece of bacon.

She accepted it and the cup of coffee that followed. "It's not cinnamon-bun," he said, "but I figured if it was in your cabinet, you'd drink it."

"Is that what you do, Lieutenant? Take a woman to bed then forage for food?"

"Tell me honestly you weren't starving."

Of course she was. He stood there shirtless, for heaven's sake. But he'd been talking about bacon, right? *The man fixed breakfast for her*. So maybe he wasn't perfect. He clearly sucked at bowing out of a one-night stand.

His problem, not hers.

Whatever.

He watched her stare at his chest.

"I admit I might be starving."

His grin suggested she'd said the absolute wrong thing, but she couldn't deny it, however he wanted to take it. Let him gloat. Anything to drive that wedge between them so she could get on with her life.

She sipped her drink while he put the last of the bacon in the pan. The grease popped but if it hit him he didn't flinch. Of course not. He probably couldn't feel anything through that set of abs. It was like armor sitting there, his skin soft but the muscle beneath it rock hard. A shiver touched her spine when she remembered that body moving over hers. And inside. She'd never felt anything like him. Thick and hot, pumping and driving and grinding and—

"You are the cutest shade of red right now."

That only made her flush more, she was sure. It was a

good thing he didn't know what she was thinking. Only he probably did.

"There's a department picnic Saturday," he said. "Any chance you'd be willing to go with me?"

She had to count to three. Then ten more.

He failed harder at one-night stands than anyone she knew. Frustrated, she blurted, "What are we doing here, Shane? You're leaving, we just had a ridiculous amount of sex, you make my bed and fix breakfast, and now you want to go on a *picnic*?" It all sounded way too quaint, even for her, a self-professed small-town girl.

He rested a hand on his hip, drawing her attention to a V-line that could have cut butter. "And what, exactly, is wrong with that?"

He had a lot of nerve accusing her of being difficult. Was the man *blind*? "Mostly the part where you're leaving," she said.

A flicker of a shadow darkened his eyes, and then it was gone. "You're new here, and you're fighting technology with that business of yours. I can introduce you to people, maybe help forge a connection or two. Once you're in with that crowd, you're family. They'll do anything in the world to help you succeed."

She drew a steady breath. Maybe she'd overreacted— apparently there really was no limit to the number of mortifying moments a person could have—but her point was no less valid for it. And why was he trying to sell her on a *family* from which he couldn't wait to escape? "If that's how you feel about this place, then why are you leaving?"

He blinked, then looked away, dredging the last of the bacon from the pan. He moved the cookware from the burner and turned off the heat before he replied. "My dad was a legend in Denver and he died a hero. I'm his son. I belong there. I can keep that alive, and I can save the next guy. It's what I was meant to do."

"Shane, you're doing that *here*."

"*Here*, I walk people across bridges." She winced at his tone, the way it suggested rescuing her was the dumbest thing he'd ever done. "I let the kids at the elementary schools see the fire engines. I get cats out of trees, and I'm not even sure why, because people are supposed to call tree companies for that. I'm meant for more."

She crossed her arms and stared him down. "You're everything in the world for that person who got her cat back."

He gave a half shrug. "Maybe. But not every firefighter who loves his job wants to go into those high-rises. Me, I crave it. *That's* where I belong."

Well, all righty then. She wouldn't be the one to argue. Not even for amazing sex. That had to be a fluke. The next time might suck, and she'd take her memories just the way he'd left them, thank you. Instead, she said, "I think I need a cat."

His lips quirked on the verge of a smile. "Single librarian with a cat. That's one for the Tinder profile."

She *really* hoped the intensity of the dirty look she'd given him had upped a notch. "If I had one such profile, and I don't, but if I ever did, which I won't, I think I'd have to lead with that thing I did with my tongue that made you say filthy things."

The smile faltered, his gaze darkening a hitch.

His reaction shouldn't have felt as good as it did, especially considering she wasn't sure what it meant. She only knew that she'd wiped that smug grin off his face by making him think about her with someone else.

As if.

She'd have ten cats before she could even think about not thinking about him.

She sighed. He had a point about introducing her to

people, and she'd be stupid to turn down that chance. "Do you really want me to go with you to the picnic? Because if it's just a post-sex parting gift—"

He pressed a kiss to her earlobe, then whispered, "I want you there. And also here. And possibly in another elevator."

She smiled, because that was the thing to do, but she couldn't help feeling melancholy. Because he could name all the places in the world, and one thing still wouldn't change.

He didn't want her enough to stay.

And if she ever wanted to get past this, she'd have to hold him to that.

• • •

Picnic day was bright and beautiful, hot but not unbearably so. Caitlin's sister would have elbowed her and suggested maybe the firemen would cope with the heat by stripping themselves of their shirts, and Caitlin would have rolled her eyes and claimed she wasn't interested.

Today, that would be a lie. At least when it came to one particular man.

And it was Lexi's elbow jostling Caitlin's ribs. "You're staring. It's almost adorable."

"Only almost?"

Lexi nudged her sunglasses and crossed her arms. "You know darn well what's under that shirt, so the gawking is almost like bragging."

Caitlin sorely hoped that was a generic accusation, because if Lexi could look at her and tell she'd had sex with Shane, that meant Caitlin had it *bad*. Unfortunately, knowing better hadn't kept her from coveting every inch of that man's body, and she wasn't sure if she'd want to forget it if she could.

But it wasn't just the sex. There was another connection that went deeper, and she couldn't put her finger on what it was, or why. Just that he wasn't so easy to dismiss, and already it hurt like hell.

Not exactly a topic for a picnic. Instead, Caitlin gave Lexi a side eye. "I'm surprised you tore your eyes off Matt long enough to notice."

Lexi's brow lifted. "No denial of the gawking, and expert deflection. Color me impressed."

"My gawking time has a definite expiration date, so I need to enjoy it while I can. What's *your* excuse?"

Lexi blinked. "Excuse for what?"

"Staring at Matt."

Lexi seemed taken aback, like she genuinely didn't realize she watched him. Then she said, "There's a whole legion of gorgeous men out there. I'm going to look. He just keeps getting in the way."

Caitlin doubted the validity of that excuse, but she was one to talk. She hadn't taken her eyes off Shane, even as she struggled with a way to get over him before she dug herself any deeper.

She was almost grateful when Lexi changed the subject. "I have an idea for your bookstore grand opening."

Shane snatched a Frisbee from an impossible height and released it in a perfect throw. "If it involves half-naked firemen," Caitlin said, "I wouldn't expect people to notice the books."

Lexi turned away from the game, and Caitlin followed as she meandered across the lawn. The sun-warmed grass tickled her toes. Shouts of children playing made her miss her sister and her nephew.

"No," Lexi said. "Far less creative than that, I'm afraid. More like, talk to the shops on either side and do a joint promo. Free scoop of ice cream with a purchase of a children's book, or, like, buy an encyclopedia and get a free cup of espresso so you can stay awake long enough to read it."

Caitlin laughed. "I don't think even that would get anyone to read an encyclopedia, but I like the idea. I'm not sure I can afford to cover the cost of the freebies, though."

"Just talk to the shops on either side. They'd probably love to help you out. Traffic from your place will almost certainly spill over to theirs, especially if you hold this event in the evening. That whole area is packed every night of the week. It's definitely a win-win. In fact, if you want me there to break the ice on that conversation, just name the time. We all go way back."

"Who goes way back?" Caitlin jumped at Shane's voice, then shivered when he put his arms around her from behind. She was also back to wanting to kick him, because she didn't need her nipples tight and her ovaries erupting in full view of the fire department.

Let alone in front of Lexi's watchful gaze.

"The majority of the people who live in this town," Lexi said, arching an eyebrow. "PDA much?"

Shane had stepped around Caitlin, relieving her of one ache and adding a hundred more. She was ruined.

Stupid bridge. She hated it times ten. "Did I not just see you on the other side of the field?" Caitlin asked.

"I'm fast," he said. "Besides, small field. Small town."

"Not so small," Lexi said. "Just not Denver. Besides, there's something here you won't find there."

It took Lexi's knowing glance in Caitlin's direction for her to understand she was the *something* in question. Her attention skated Shane's way in time to catch him falter, the cocky smile wavering for a split second before it rallied.

As much as she hated men who were full of themselves, she'd grown to love that smile. The first version, that was. Not the forced one he'd just thrown back.

"He'll have an endless supply of women to rescue," Caitlin said. "I'm pretty sure that's a plus."

Lexi gave him a pointed look. "And here we were all thinking he'd finally rescued one worth hanging on to."

Oh Lord. Caitlin had to be redder than the fire engines parked in a line along one side of the road. A green expanse of parkland stretched between the bulk of the revelers and the department vehicles, though a convoy of small children stood in rapt attention around a couple of guys in turnout gear, the group inching the length of the ladder truck as the men likely introduced them its various parts and functions.

That group aside, most everyone congregated by the river. From this angle, it was the bridge that seemed imposing, towering high above the rushing current in a twisted formation of steel and concrete. The water, with sunlight glistening off the current, was no longer a dark abyss, but an endless, artistic play of light. Which didn't keep her breath from catching when one of the children wandered near, despite the adults who stuck close.

Shane still hadn't responded to Lexi's teasing. Nope, he waited until the non-answer became conspicuous, until Caitlin glanced back at him, to capture her gaze and say, "She's hard to hold."

Lexi's eyes widened as Caitlin's narrowed.

He shrugged. "Tickle spots," he said with a grin.

Caitlin was spared a response—hers or Lexi's—when Matt approached. "Waffles is about to pull my arm off."

Caitlin and Shane exchanged glances, until Shane said to Matt, "I don't see a dog."

"He was with a group of kids while we played Frisbee," he said, "and when I took him, he insisted on stopping and getting his head scratched by everyone we passed. Fortunately, Diego saw me surrounded with throngs of women and made a comment about how the dog was a chick magnet, so I handed him the leash. As soon as he figures out they were all there for me, not the dog, he'll be looking to hand it back. And that's where you come in."

Lexi rolled her eyes. "I'll get the dog," she said. "Maybe you should catch up with thc *throngs*."

"I hate to break it to you," Shane said to Matt as Lexi stalked off. "But I'm pretty sure it's the dog."

Matt grinned. "I know. But Diego needs to get out there. His divorce was finalized months ago."

"And it'll take a lot longer than that to want to take a chance on trusting someone again," Shane said. For Caitlin, he added, "His wife cheated on him."

"Ouch." Caitlin winced, though the obvious disapproval the men shared settled warmly inside her. Not that it meant anything. Shane was committed to being non-committed in another town. There was nothing for her to think about.

Matt leveled a gaze on Caitlin and Shane. "You never know. Once he sees you settling down…"

"I'm not settling," Shane said, causing that ache in Caitlin's chest to twist.

"No, you're not," Matt said, giving Caitlin a warm smile. "But *she* sure as hell is if she puts up with your ass. Anyway, I'm off to find the hot dog vendor. I can't eat anything with that mutt around. Big pleading eyes get me every time."

"Noted," Shane said. "Remind me never to look at you that way."

"I learned to ignore your eyelash batting years ago," Matt said with a laugh. As he walked off, Shane took Caitlin's hand.

For a moment she thought he was being nice, but then she realized they were headed toward the river.

She ground to a halt. "Absolutely not."

"I promise you'll be okay. There are dozens of firemen and women here along with half the town. If I let you fall in, I'd never live it down."

She mock-glared as the sentiment turned into teasing arrogance. "Just for that, I should *jump* in."

He spun her behind a tree, the truck a barrier between them and the rest of the picnic. "And I would go in after you." He grazed her mouth with a soft kiss. "As often as I had to." The next kiss was deeper, softer. She put her hands against his chest, half intending to push him away, but she ended up clutching his shirt and dragging him a notch closer.

In spite of that, she managed to whisper, "Aren't you supposed to behave?" Thank God for the tree at her back. Not so much for the man teasing her with his mouth, alternating between nipping at her lip and pressing deeper, turning her into a squiggly mess.

"No one is within fifty yards of us," he said, "and this tree and that little bit of brush behind it is blocking all of my misbehavior. Any more excuses?"

"Only that you're a lieutenant and probably should be some kind of example when in the company of your entire department and half the city."

He grinned. "I am on my best behavior."

She took her sweet time extracting herself from the next kiss. "This is you behaving?"

"It's the consequence of it. Not touching you is driving me crazy."

"I hope Denver knows what's coming, then."

His grin faltered. He took a step back, eliciting a pang from her chest that promised more in the coming weeks. But the moment passed, and before that lump in her throat could fully form, he'd managed to lose the darkest corners of his expression and snag her hand.

She didn't ask what happened, or what he'd been thinking. She just let it go.

She needed the practice.

With the moment drifting behind them on a light breeze, she followed him, fingers laced, the gesture feeling a lot more complicated than it looked on the surface. It was so casual, something boyfriends did. But he wasn't her boyfriend. He wasn't hers at all. But it belied a certain intimacy—one that may have existed, at least in terms of physical familiarity, but wasn't something she'd expect him to advertise.

Lost in thought, trailing a step behind on the narrow path, she let her focus drift to the planes of his back where his damp tee clung to his muscles, and didn't realize they'd reached the river until he stopped. She balked a step behind him, but a gentle tug at her hand had her standing at his side.

"I've got you," he said. "The curve in the river here means the water is almost still. I thought you might want to put your toes in."

"You thought wrong." She only had half a fight in her. The truth was she *did* trust him. She just wasn't sure she wanted to add this to the list of things for which she'd forever remember him. Water was a pretty broad, damning category.

He laughed, then caught sight of her face and quickly sobered. "I'm not discounting your fear. I get it. But this is one step I know you can take."

She worried her lip, grappling with the truth. She had no reason to tell him. He'd be out of her life as quickly as he entered it, but she still needed him to understand. "When I was a teenager," she explained, "I was in the truck with my parents and my sister and a flash flood hit from a storm in the next county. The water came out of nowhere. No storm clouds. Just moonlight on all that churning water and the feeling of the truck being carried away. I still can't look at rushing water."

"Was anyone hurt?"

She forced a smile. "Just my lasting psychological damage."

"But you made it, sweetheart," he said tenderly. "As bad as that was, you survived. This is nothing. You can do this."

"Or I could live my entire life and never touch this water."

"*Or*," he argued gently, "you could live the rest of your life knowing you stepped out of your comfort zone and into this river."

"What does it matter to you?" As soon as she asked, she realized the answer. Another notch in his hero totem pole.

But nothing in his expression supported that. Sincerity touched his eyes when he told her, "Because when I think of you, I want to know you conquered your biggest fear."

He'd rather associate her with a river than sex that had actually knocked plaster off the wall? She could have kicked herself for the way that irritated her. "What if it's not my biggest fear?" she asked. What if her biggest fear was *him*? And the way he made her feel.

The fact that he'd soon be gone.

"Then you have no excuse." He toed off his shoes then tugged off his socks. A couple of rolls to his department-issue pant legs later, he'd stepped into the water. It barely rippled around his ankles. "See? Nothing to it. You've got this."

Her heart hammered, but she kicked off her sandals and took a tentative step in. The ice-cold water took her breath.

Or maybe it was him.

The current lapped at her feet, where sunlight danced on the surface above her toes. He took her hand and held tightly, offering reassurance that in no way should have come from him. She'd have better luck holding onto water through her open palm than she would Shane, but her heart still felt the warmth.

Traitor.

"You're fine," he said.

She forced a smile. It came easier this time than most. "Of course I am. I'm standing in two inches of water."

He grinned. "Want to go deeper?"

"No way." But wasn't she? By the freaking millisecond. Fortunately, her stomach growled, saving her the indignity of examining that thought. Even if he stayed in Dry Rock, he wasn't what she wanted. He wanted to fix her, and she thought she was just fine how she was.

Mostly.

She really needed to get her mind off him and back on her work. She had a store to open and Lexi's offer to help, which took the edge off approaching the adjacent shop owners. Already, she felt more pulled together.

Except with Shane. He pulled her apart.

He let her go. It probably had more to do with the fact that she stood in two inches of water—which, river aside, wasn't any huge accomplishment—and was less of a symbolic gesture, but she felt the sting of the symbolism all the same.

"You did it," he said.

She wasn't sure how she felt about the pride in his voice. "There are toddlers fifty yards downstream who are also doing it."

"But they're not doing it as awesomely as you are," he said, cupping a hand to the back of her head and pulling her toward him for a kiss.

"Those less awesome toddlers and their parents can see you," she said against his mouth.

"Damned dress code. Makes me too easy to recognize." He shook his head good-naturedly and stepped out of the water. He slid back into his shoes and socks, and she, her sandals. "I'm starving. Want to check out the food?"

"Sure." Actually, she was a bit nervous about joining the thick of the crowd. She'd said hello to plenty of people, and Lexi had introduced her around, but that was without Shane. With him, the muddled state of their not-a-relationship took a front seat, and not even she knew what to think.

Especially not after he took her hand and walked directly toward a throng of fifty or more people, as if he wanted everyone to assume they were together when he'd made it clear *she* couldn't even assume as much.

The food tables were packed. Served buffet style, with a lot of meat. Typical man-centric kind of thing, she supposed.

Shane paused near a pile of what looked like breaded, kettle-cooked potato chips and gave her a devilish grin. "Ever had Rocky Mountain Oysters?" he asked.

A man behind Caitlin cleared his throat. "Son, if she eats one of those without knowing what they are, Denver won't be far enough for you to escape."

Shane laughed and shook hands with whoever it was. "Chief Holloway," he said, "Meet Caitlin Tyler, new proprietor of Shelf Indulgence. Caitlin, this is the chief. Has been for as long as I can remember."

Caitlin took in his friendly smile and grandfatherly salt-and-pepper hair and immediately liked him. He took and patted her hand, cocking his head toward Shane. "Shame to lose this one," he said. "Damned shame."

"Andrew, watch your language." A woman with kind eyes and a playfully disapproving frown leaned in and chided him. "And this must be Caitlin. It's so nice to meet you."

"Elizabeth Holloway," Shane said. "The woman who keeps the chief in line."

"No small feat," she said with a smile, "but landing this guy?" She looked toward Shane. "Now *that* is an accomplishment."

Caitlin just stood there, battling feelings of embarrassment and the urge to flee. She'd worried she and Shane might give the wrong impression by coming together to the picnic, but she'd let that be his call. She had no idea the rumors had flowed *this* fast and hard.

And now two very nice-seeming people were looking at her like she'd pulled some kind of miracle. "Seems Dry Rock might have an edge on Denver after all," the chief said.

It would have been a *big* miracle, had she pulled it off.

"It's so nice to meet you both," Caitlin said, ignoring the shadow that crossed Shane's face at the chief's words. Did he hate being linked with her that much? He couldn't, because he'd insisted. She figured she'd get him alone and ask him, or at least find out if he wanted her to bail, but she didn't get the chance.

The chief's radio squawked. Shane and a couple of the firemen who stood nearby paused long enough to listen, then the majority of them—chief included—jumped into action, saying good-byes and disposing of food plates.

"Got a call," Shane said. "It's my shift." He dropped a kiss on her mouth before he took off with the rest of them. She watched as several pieces of equipment peeled from the line, sirens blaring. A number of department members hung back, undeployed, but the mood had shifted.

Once the vehicles had disappeared in the direction of the highway, many of the families left behind began to pack up picnic blankets and lawn chairs. Caitlin turned back to the chief's wife. "What, exactly, is a Rocky Mountain Oyster?"

"Calf testicles," she said. "Sliced and deep fried."

"I would have killed him," Caitlin said, side-eyeing Lexi, who had just joined them with an enormous dog attached by a leash.

"And he'd have come back for more," Lexi said.

"Is that a horse?" Caitlin asked, ignoring the commentary about Shane.

"Nah. It's just Waffles. He's a mastiff. And a pain in the butt. I need to get him home before he takes out you, me, and every bite of food left on the table. Otherwise, I'd help you stay and clean up." She directed the last part toward Mrs. Holloway.

"No need to remind me," the older woman said with a laugh. "That was the most memorable Christmas parade yet. My granddaughters still ask about the dog that knocked over

Santa."

"Not just Santa," Lexi said. "The whole sleigh."

"The sleigh?" Caitlin repeated.

"Yes," Mrs. Holloway said. "And guess who was in it, playing Santa?"

"Chief Holloway?" Caitlin asked.

"None other."

Lexi laughed, though it was interrupted by a fierce tug on the leash. "He still reminds me of that moment every chance he gets."

"I would, too," Caitlin said. "You go. I'll help with the food." She was grateful to have something to do. Something other than trying to figure out this dead-end thing with Shane, which in and of itself was a dead-end thing. She sighed. "If you can use my help, that is."

"That would be lovely," Mrs. Holloway said. "To be honest, I'm dying to find out how you snagged that man."

"Aren't we all," Lexi said with a snort. "I'm out of here before this turns into a Shirley MacLaine incident." No sooner than the words left her mouth, the dog took off, nearly dragging Lexi.

"Good luck," Caitlin called after her.

"She needs your luck," Mrs. Holloway said. "That Shane, he's as sweet as can be. Great at his job, of course, but he's never kept a woman around long. He's always wanting to move on to greener pastures."

Sweet? Ha. Okay, maybe a little, but greener pastures? Oddly, the same thing his friends had accused him of that night she'd been introduced to them at the diner. Caitlin frowned. "I doubt there are many pastures in Denver."

Mrs. Holloway *tsk*ed. "He misses his dad. He truly was a hero and he died that way. We all felt that loss, even before we knew the family, but I don't think anyone felt it like Shane did."

"How long ago did it happen?" Caitlin wanted to know—wanted him to be okay—even though it only dragged her deeper into this world that only pretended to be hers.

Mrs. Holloway halted her cleanup, staring momentarily toward the sky. "Twenty years now, I think it's been."

Shane would have been about ten then. Several yards away, a little boy, half that, ran and leaped into the arms of a man wearing a fire department shirt. A woman stood nearby, a toddler on her hip, beaming at the pair.

Caitlin couldn't imagine that kind of loss.

"It's a dangerous job," Mrs. Holloway said, following Caitlin's gaze, "but they take so many precautions. I think a lot of us on the back lines are lulled into a comfort zone. These men and women are heroes. To our children, they're invincible. It's impossible to imagine the worst that could happen, and when it does, it's not something you ever really get over."

"What happened to Shane's dad?" Caitlin asked.

"There was a fire in a high-rise. The building was supposedly clear, but Shane's dad swore he saw someone in an upper window. Half the crew argued with him, but he wouldn't listen. Went right back up those stairs and found a young woman. He managed to point her in the direction of a fire escape, she said, but he couldn't get through the same hole in his gear, so he radioed down that he was taking the stairs. That was the last anyone heard from him. There had been a partial collapse inside, and he was pinned."

Caitlin felt something hot and wet on her cheek and found herself wiping away a tear. Shane's words from the day her air conditioner caught fire came back to her. *And then the goddamned ceiling collapses.* He'd startled her then with the sharp words. Now, she understood.

"That woman would have died without him," Mrs. Holloway continued. "I understand Shane wanting to make that kind of difference. Everyone in the department does. But he needs to fill that hole in himself before he runs off to save an entire city. His father's legacy isn't in Denver. It's inside Shane. I hoped he'd figure that out before he left us." She smiled and patted Caitlin on the shoulder. "I'm glad he found you."

"I'm not sure he has," Caitlin stammered.

Mrs. Holloway handed Caitlin a plate and piled it high with barbecue and coleslaw. "You haven't been here long enough to see the difference in him," she said. "The rest of us...well, I'd just about given up, but maybe it's not too late after all."

Chapter Sixteen

Shane felt bad for leaving Caitlin like he had, but she seemed to have taken it in stride. The call—an overturned tanker on the interstate—had tied them up for hours dealing with HAZMAT. Anything involving hazardous materials usually did. Fortunately, there hadn't been any injuries and what had amounted to a minor spill had been contained to the pavement, saving the area from significant environmental impact.

Back at the station, he'd debated contacting Caitlin, but he didn't know what to say…not that that stopped him from thinking about her all night. Now, it was Sunday. He reported to his new job in eight days, and he still hadn't checked on that apartment, the idea of which suddenly seemed lonely.

He wanted to call Caitlin, to lose himself in her, but he needed to think.

He *needed* to figure out who he was without her, because he didn't recognize that guy anymore. He'd been a little too comfortable with her at the picnic. Being with her felt natural, like something that just fit right, and it wasn't until he and the guys were standing around at the scene, waiting for HAZMAT to do its job, that he realized how much had changed.

He missed her.

Caitlin felt *right*.

She had to be wondering why he hadn't called, but how could he explain that she scared the hell out of him? He had never seen himself settling down—couldn't imagine having a wife and kids waiting at home to get that call they got when his dad died. That was why he kept things casual, but she'd slipped through whatever defenses he'd once harbored. There'd been fireworks, yeah. But after the explosions calmed and the sparks fell, in the quiet of her bedroom or in the aftermath of an elevator tryst, there was something between them he'd never fully experienced.

Contentment.

He couldn't remember a moment in his life when he wasn't mentally plotting his next step. As a kid, he'd just wanted to be like his dad. He spent his high school years gearing up to pursue fire science, then he'd done that and signed on with the department and begun to climb the ladder. That singular focus had been there since the first time he'd stepped into his dad's boots. His mom had a twenty-eight-year-old picture of him teetering in the oversize boots, a great big smile and a smudge of dirt on his face. That was probably Shane's oldest memory.

And wasn't that the gist of it? He'd been driven to this since he was in diapers. No one but Caitlin had ever made him want anything else, but how could he explain that to her? *You make me want too much.*

For any other man, that wouldn't be a flaw.

It would mean the world.

She would *be* the world.

It was a balmy night, perfect for a ride through the mountains, but instead he ended up at the diner, where he sat outside for a few minutes. Even though he'd been hanging out there with the guys for the better part of ten years, everything about the place now reminded him of Caitlin. At this point, he worried everything would.

He might as well eat.

Sighing, he parked the bike, stowed his helmet, and fed a meter. He didn't need to see the municipal lot or think of how he'd felt when she'd slid her arms around him and held on, much less what had happened thereafter.

She'd changed him, and he didn't know his way back.

When he walked in, he found the crew at the usual spot. Lexi was glaring at Matt about who-knew-what-now. Jack and Diego had given them some distance, splitting the table and leaving a wide swath of red vinyl between the two sides.

"Thank God," Jack said when he saw Shane. "We look like a couple over here."

"You don't have to sit that close," Shane said, a forced attempt at joining the fray. "People will talk."

"Let them," Diego said. "It's better than giving Lexi easy access to my fries."

At the mention of her name, Lexi twisted in her seat to give Diego a dirty look. "I only take the ones you complain about."

"You complained about fries?" Shane asked. God, it was good to be back with them. Nothing heavy happening there... just the usual bullshit.

"He said they were too hot," Lexi explained.

"I *think* I could have waited a moment for them to cool off and they'd have been just fine," Diego told her.

Lexi ignored him, turning instead to Shane. "Where's Caitlin?"

He shrugged. "Unpacking, I guess." Whether she was working late at the store or sitting at home, the same was probably true. He thought about the boxes still scattered about her house, about how she was moving forward. About how he felt stuck.

"I hope you're taking the boxes for the big move," Jack said.

"Or maybe he's decided he's not going," Lexi said. "Did you not talk to her?"

"I don't have much to pack," Shane said, ignoring the latter question. He figured he'd settle in, then come back one weekend and figure out what to do with the house and its contents, most of which he didn't need in a furnished apartment.

"You leave Dry Rock," Lexi said, "you'll have even less."

"He's a grown man, not a stupid kid," Matt said. "He's not going to change his life over a woman he's known less than two weeks."

Lexi glared. "You think he's not *going* to change?" She waved her arm at him, like he was part of the showcase showdown on *The Price is Right*. "He already has. Look at him."

"Look at me?" Shane asked. He glanced down at his shirt and back again. "What does that mean?"

Jack rubbed his hand against his chin. "I see what you're saying."

Diego nodded. "Pathetic."

Matt sat back and shook his head, like he thought they were all ridiculous. At least Shane had one friend in the group, unless Matt was just doing that to irritate Lexi.

Probably.

Shane sighed. "Matt's right. Nothing changes."

"And you're wrong," Lexi said. "It's already changed. Take off in a week. Be an ass then if you must, but why waste the time you have left?"

Because he'd already had a hole in his life he couldn't fill. Because digging another one would be torture.

But so was good-bye. And goddamn, so was the weight of regrets.

He at least owed Caitlin an explanation. Things had gone too far between them to walk away without that much, even if he wasn't sure how to convey his need to go, much less reconcile it with leaving. But he had to do that.

He had to let go. He'd waited his whole life for the chance.

Lexi was in the throes of staring him down when he waved over the waitress. "Can I get a chocolate milkshake and some fries to go?" he asked. His question earned an approving smile, so that was something. He just hoped Caitlin would see things the same way, because *I care enough to tell you I don't care enough to stay* wasn't his best line.

Not that it mattered. Staying had never been an option.

"Didn't I see you come up on the bike?" Jack asked. "I know you think you have mad skills, but road grit in the food isn't cool, man."

"A milkshake with a lid," Shane amended. "And a bag for the fries."

The waitress left with his order.

"Milkshake with a lid?" Diego laughed. "You'll crush the whipped cream."

"Yeah," Matt said, waggling his brow. "That stuff might come in handy."

Lexi rolled her eyes. "I can't imagine why you came here to begin with, knowing she's at home alone, but if it doesn't work out, you know we'll be here for you."

Yeah, he did.

For about a week.

Then he was on his own.

• • •

Caitlin was curled up on her sofa, air conditioning cranked

up to comfort-clothing weather. Her leggings and chunky sweater hadn't quite fixed things this time, but she burrowed into their familiarity anyway. Ice cream would have made a fantastic companion.

So would a certain lieutenant.

At least she had Netflix, even if she lacked the chill. She'd had to Google that one, and no wonder brick-and-mortar stores were going out of business. If she had a choice, no doubt what she'd have been doing right then.

And no matter how many batteries he'd bought her, the solo version didn't count.

They should have had more time. In the space of a single department picnic invitation, he'd killed the notion of a one-night stand and had gone public with their relationship, however he quantified it. To have kissed her in front of the chief and the rest of the department only to literally walk out of her life didn't seem fair. But neither did putting off the inevitable. She wasn't sure which option would be harder, but he hadn't given her a choice. That wasn't easy to live with, either.

Somehow, she'd expected more.

A hard knock sounded at the door, and she nearly jumped out of her skin. She didn't know anyone who'd come to her house except Shane or Lexi. Lexi had invited her to hang out, but on the chance Shane might be there, Caitlin had declined. She wasn't ready to say good-bye in public, though she supposed she already had at the picnic. She just hadn't realized it at the time.

And still, she had no clue what had happened. Under other circumstances she would have checked in later that evening without giving it a second thought, but she hadn't, because she didn't know how long they'd be on the call. By morning, she realized she wasn't going to hear anything at all.

She'd yet to figure out why she cared.

She'd equally failed to stop caring.

She peeked outside, wondering if maybe a neighbor had stopped by. Caitlin had spent very little time at her house, and it didn't look much different than when the truck had been unloaded. The bookstore took priority.

Yep, that was the plan. Lose herself in the store. Definitely not…

Shane.

Her breath lodged in her throat. Steadying herself didn't work, so she gave up and opened the door.

He didn't wait for an invitation. He just barged in, shoving a cup and a bag in her arms as he passed, all without saying a word. For the longest moment she could only gawk as he stood there, breathing hard, pacing the short length of her kitchen while she stood next to an open door, letting in every fly in the neighborhood, as her grandmother would have said.

She nudged the door until the latch *snick*ed, then peered in the bag. Fries. The cup held a milkshake, still too thick to pour, so she scooped some up with her finger and licked it clean.

He watched, heat radiating.

The man was a sadist.

And sexy as hell.

He drove his fingers uselessly through his hair. Muscles flexed under his shirt, and the way his thighs shaped his jeans made her think way too hard about his thrusting skills.

Yeah, he needed to go. "We need—"

"I don't know why this had to happen," he interrupted, his voice anguished enough to tear at her heart. "Everything was settled. I had a plan. I had everything I wanted, damn it, and now all I can think about is you. What book you're reading. What else you're afraid of." He stopped. Took a breath that made his chest quiver. "Who you'll be with when I'm gone."

Was he really thinking about her *being with* someone else? She wanted to let him, if that's what he wanted to do, but was that what he really thought of her? If so, she'd give him a hell of a lot more than her silence on the matter.

"Shane—"

She didn't get a chance to finish, because he'd stalked the distance between them, sparks flying from the heat in his eyes. She might have melted on the spot if he hadn't pinned her against the wall, fire fueling the kiss that made her forget about the food and the six days they had left and the fact that he really, really sucked at good-byes. Because this wasn't letting go. This was taking everything she had left and making a knot of it.

"We're going to talk," he said, the words as tender as his kisses were demanding. "But right now I need you. I need to know you're real."

She nodded, tears threatening, and she wasn't sure why. His intensity caught her off guard. Made her admit, if only to herself, that this wasn't something she'd invented in her head...that they had something—however inconvenient—that was worth fighting for.

At least for the night.

He scooped her into his arms. Glancing at her legs, he shook his head. "I don't know where you shop," he said, "but damned if I've ever been there."

"Like you'd wander through the women's leggings section of any store." Yeah, they could just discuss her clothes. With everything else between them, *that* made sense.

He carried her down the hall, her heart out-thumping his every footfall. She braced herself for the playful impact of hitting the sheets, but instead of tossing her on the bed, he eased her to her feet then peeled back the covers while she set the food aside.

Shane didn't seem the least bit concerned with it getting cold or melty. She wasn't even sure he noticed it in the dim light, because he was too busy stripping her of the sweater, then his borrowed shirt she wore underneath.

"Damn, you're beautiful." He gently tugged her hair from its ponytail, and dropped to his knees to help her step out of her pants.

Which left her, once again, the only naked person in the room.

He pulled off his shirt while she worked on his jeans. He let her unbutton and unzip but stopped her from taking him into her hands. "Not yet, sweetheart." He shed the rest of his clothing then walked her to the bed. He managed to roll on a condom he got from who-knew-where and then crawled into bed with her. A touch of his fingers told him she was ready. Embarrassingly so, she thought, especially since ten minutes ago she'd been alone, thinking she'd never see him again.

Now, he was destroying her.

He threaded his fingers through her hair and captured her gaze as he entered her, the moment so terrifyingly intimate that she couldn't breathe. She'd never felt so close to someone. She'd never been so *afraid*.

Her eyes fluttered closed, but he whispered her name, *Caitlin*, and brought her back to him. He was so thick, filled her so completely, that she thought she might burst and die from the pleasure, but this time the intimacy wasn't between the sheets.

It was the eye contact.

Over and over, he found the deepest part of her. It went beyond physical, beyond laced fingers and a cocoon of sheets to something she'd never experienced. Never dreamed.

She wouldn't have called the wild, wall-shattering sex they'd shared the first time fucking, and she wasn't sure she'd downgrade this to *just sex*. It was different.

It was a connection she didn't know how to break.

But she'd learn.

She'd have to.

Chapter Seventeen

Caitlin woke before the sun, the emptiness hitting her before the realization that Shane was gone. Had he slept at all, or had he bailed when she'd drifted off? The cool sheets offered no answers. Just the sharpening edge of heartbreak and a growing realization that the melted milkshake, cold fries, and abandoned shirt were all he'd left her of this thing they had. Or didn't have, it seemed.

She'd known it was coming, so why did it hurt so much?

Because you're falling in love with him, you idiot.

She'd put up a hell of a fight, using logic and reason once the orgasms clouded her view, but it hadn't mattered. He'd pushed past all of it, finding a place in her heart that had never belonged to anyone else, and with her luck, probably never would.

And on the heels of *that*, he'd run. He might be running toward something, but she didn't buy for a moment that there wasn't a part of him running from *her*.

Damned if she'd make it easy.

His new job meant something to him. She got that. But

what they had meant something, too. Something that deserved a chance. She'd never ask him to stay, but that didn't mean she wanted to let him go. A long distance relationship sounded like the worst idea in the world—especially when she wanted nothing more than to spend every night in his arms—but people had sacrificed far more than living a couple of hours apart. They could do weekends. They could try.

They had better options than a middle-of-the-night disappearance. He owed her more.

She owed *herself* more than letting him get away with that.

That determination carried her to the firehouse, the bridge barely registering as it glided past her Uber window. If only Shane could be so easy to forget.

She hesitated at the front door of the station. Should she knock, or was this a public building kind of thing where she should just walk in? She opted for a closer examination of the doorway, hoping to find a buzzer, but before one materialized, the door opened.

Not Shane.

It was Jack, and he didn't hide his surprise. "Come on in, Caitlin. I'll let him know you're here."

She followed him past a small office to an open living area, where she took in a massive flat-screen television. Across from it sat the tattered remains of a sofa that looked like it had come from a frat house. Leather recliners dominated the rest of the room, which was otherwise clean and sparsely decorated. A PA system let off a few random tones, but nothing that seemed to spur anyone there into action.

She didn't have to wait long before Shane appeared. "Hey," he said. "What's up?"

Well, that was…the exact opposite of deeply personal. He wanted to put distance between them—that much was clear. But he didn't get to spend those hours looking at her like that, touching her, and just walk away.

"You left without saying good-bye," she told him.

His stare was blank, bordering on cold. She didn't buy it for a moment, but he wanted her to, and that sucked. "Leaving *was* good-bye," he said.

"That's not you," she said. "You don't run from things." Never mind that she'd already decided he was doing that very thing. She wasn't going to let him push her away that easily.

His dark eyes rested heavily on her. "No, I run toward them. You knew that going in."

Going in. Like this was some experience she could have anticipated. Something she'd signed up for. She stifled a humorless laugh. "I might be learning," she said. "To do that, I mean." Standing here, she realized she'd have to. This wasn't the man who'd made love to her all night. This was the morning-after version who wanted to shrug off a good time and move on.

"Explain," he said.

His wariness gave her second thoughts, but then the memories took over, her lip throbbing where he'd bitten it, her body aching when he'd let her go. And she knew, no matter how vulnerable it left her, she had to say what she felt. "I'm…falling in love with you."

He stared, his expression blank. She'd love to get behind that, to know what he might be thinking, but he didn't give her an inch, so she pushed ahead.

"I've— I've never been more afraid of anything in my life." She stammered at first, but then the words came fast, like she had to get them out there or they'd stay stuck, forever. "I know it's soon," she added, "but there's something between us. I don't think we should give it up. The last thing I wanted was a long distance relationship…at least until it came to a choice between that and losing you, and I'm not ready to do that yet."

He just stood there for the longest time, a war waging in his eyes. One that she was suddenly terrified she'd find herself on the losing side of.

"Caitlin, I can't."

She blinked.

"You of all people should understand," he said. "You wanted something—you wanted that bookstore—and you went for it. You left people behind. Your parents. Your sister. You had a dream and followed it. I have no idea why it had to be *here*, but I can't let that stop *me*."

She couldn't argue his point, but that didn't make it hurt any less. The words stung, but with any luck she'd be miles from him before she broke down. "Okay," she finally said. "I should go."

He stepped back so he no longer stood between her and the exit. He seemed to hesitate, and the muscle working in his jaw further convinced her he had something he wanted to say. But he won the battle against saying it, at least until she stepped back out into the sunshine.

"This was supposed to be fun," he called after her. "No matter how hard, or how fast, it was never meant to be anything more."

The words, though she acknowledged their truth, felt like the worst lie. What this thing between them was meant to be meant nothing. Not next to what it had become.

Nothing on earth could have hidden her hurt, but she threw him a smile with absolutely no truth behind it and said, "Then rest easy, Lieutenant. Because you got your wish."

Chapter Eighteen

There were moments Shane would give anything to erase. Watching Caitlin turn on her heel and leave topped the list.

This conversation with Matt came in at a close second.

"You're fucked," Matt told him.

"That's incredibly helpful," Shane said. "And also old news." His gaze blindly traversed the printouts stuck all over his office walls. He shared the space with the lead guy on each shift, so it wasn't exactly personal, but he'd still miss it. And he'd yet to figure why he hadn't kicked Matt the hell out.

"It's not like you to get torn up over a woman," Matt said. "Level with me. What's going on?"

Shane sighed heavily. There was no way Matt would relent, but more than that, if Shane filled him in, maybe some of it would get back to Caitlin. Maybe Lexi would make sense of it for her. Maybe she'd hurt a little less. But he couldn't let Matt think he wanted him to run his mouth, so he threw out a warning he fully expected to go unheeded. All to take the coward's way out.

"Anything I say stays here," Shane said. "Never to be

repeated. Even the vaguest reference means I go straight to Lexi with the reason she had a house full of praying mantises."

Matt snickered. "Deal."

That Matt could find humor in having opened a jar of baby mantises in her house—or rather, that she might learn he'd helped along the situation—made Shane think he should talk to Diego instead. That man had been through hell with his divorce, so he of all people would get it, but he was also the last one who needed to hear it. He'd lost the woman he loved; Shane was walking away from his.

And fuck wherever that thought was headed. He picked at a chip on the desk rather than meet Matt's eyes. "I have never felt this way about a woman. Not even close. She's the most contrary person I've ever met. She has to argue or question everything I say. She's…"

"Damn near perfect for you?" Matt supplied.

Shane ignored him. "And physically…" What could he even say? "We connect. It's intense."

"Still waiting to hear the problem," Matt said, sounding bored.

A beep sounded throughout the building. Shane listened to dispatch until he was sure it was another station's call, then continued. "I've wanted this transfer for as long as I can remember. I've wanted *her* for a couple of weeks."

Matt shrugged, kicking back in a creaky pea-soup-green chair that had an inventory sticker from the nineteen-seventies stuck to the bottom. "We don't get to pick the moments that change our lives."

The words dug a little deeper than Shane would readily admit, not just in terms of Caitlin, but for his dad. He responded by shoving Matt's feet off his desk.

They hit the floor with a dull *thud*. Matt scowled. "You realize you're never going to live up to this image you've crafted in your head, right? You won't ever be him."

His dad. What Shane wouldn't give for that to be different. It would have changed so much. Too much, maybe. "You sound like my sister."

"Jess doesn't hold back. She wants you here."

"I earned that transfer," Shane said evenly, but even as the words left his mouth, he wondered. His dad's guys had stayed in touch, and their support had been steadfast for two decades now. From the time he'd joined the FD, he'd been told he had a job in Denver if he ever wanted one.

All because of his father's name.

For the first time in his life, he didn't see that as a good thing. But that didn't mean he didn't have anything to prove.

It left him with *more* to prove.

"Your dad was an in," Matt said. "I'm not saying you don't deserve the job, and I know you'd kick ass at it, but you'll be there because of him and you know it. We all know it. What the rest of us know that you don't is that he's gone."

Shane gave Matt a sharp look. "Do I punch you now, or wait until you're not expecting it?"

Matt held his arms wide. "Take your shot if you want it. You'll only prove I'm getting to you." His smile faded. "Look, you aren't your father. It doesn't matter how great he was, or how great you'll be. You're your own damn person, and if you're worried about what he'd think, I'm guessing nothing would make him prouder than to see you make your own way in this world. Love him. Remember him. Honor him. But step the fuck out of his shadow. Things don't grow in the dark." He paused. "You know what every parent seems to want?"

Shane blinked. "Do *you*?"

Matt nodded. "I think so. You'd be horrified by how much Hallmark Channel I'm forced to watch with Lexi."

"Okay, I'll bite. What does every parent want?"

"For their child to be happy."

"Not much of a revelation there," Shane said.

"Then try this one for size," Matt said. "And try not to lie to yourself. You've got Denver on one side and Caitlin on the other. Let's assume there's no compromise and that you have to pick one. Which one are you willing to live without?"

Life without Caitlin. He'd need his memories wiped to have a chance in hell for that to happen. But he'd worked too hard and for too long to give it up now. He hadn't done that for his family, and he couldn't do it for her.

He had to go to Denver.

. . .

One week later

Now that Caitlin knew what Netflix and chill was, she was surprised to have any traffic at her grand opening, but the place was jumping. When the tenth person arrived within the first hour, Caitlin and Lexi exchanged perplexed glances. Lexi shrugged. "Maybe the word got out about the sex books."

"That would *not* be ideal." Besides, she'd stashed most of those in the back. She didn't want to be run out of town for being the porn lady, though those dusty old volumes were yet another thing that didn't have anything on the internet or streaming television. "But something had to have happened. Any idea what?"

Lexi reached over to scratch the head of the fluffball of a kitten Caitlin had adopted from the shelter. "My guess? People met you and like you and they want to see you succeed, so they've all piled in here to buy books."

"That would be fantastic, but I have a feeling I'm going to end up putting a lot of these obscure books online."

"Good," Lexi said. "Go with the flow of things. That's how you succeed. And by the way, you're not fooling anyone with this cat's name."

"I don't know what you're talking about," Caitlin lied.

"Lou? Really? No relation to a certain lieutenant?"

That certain lieutenant was long gone. She hadn't seen him since the morning at the firehouse, and while she wasn't quite okay with that, she was getting there. Kitten's name notwithstanding. To Lexi, she said, "I'm certain they don't share a single strand of DNA." That much, at least, was true, if not exactly what Lexi meant.

"Good to know," Lexi said, though her tone suggested she wasn't buying it.

Caitlin pushed those thoughts away and rang up a stack of books for one customer, and then for two more customers after that. Before she stepped away from the register, a striking young woman with glossy dark hair approached. She seemed familiar, and Caitlin assumed from the picnic, until Lexi greeted her.

"Hey, Jess," Lexi said. "Have you and Caitlin met?"

"No," Jess said. "Because my brother is a moron who thinks sticking his head in the sand makes things a little less real."

Lexi offered Caitlin a bemused look. "Jess is Shane's sister. She's as blunt as he is obtuse."

"I love you already," Caitlin said. No wonder she thought Jess looked familiar. She and Shane intensely favored each other. She wanted to ask how he was, but his name on her tongue…it was still too raw. Breaking down in front of the fifteen people currently crowding her store wouldn't go over well.

Jess offered a warm smile. "Good, because that book you took to the fire station for Shane to read? If it's for sale, I'd like to buy it." Caitlin's curiosity must have been obvious, because Jess added, "I want to give it to him for his birthday."

"Now *I* love you," Lexi said. "Without even knowing the details of this plot, I'm convinced he deserves it."

"So he told you about that book?" Caitlin didn't try to

hide her surprise, though she did manage to shoot Lexi a dirty look. Surely Jess hadn't heard the sordid details of Caitlin's not-a-relationship with Shane from her brother, and Caitlin didn't want her to hear them here. Not in front of her.

"Sort of," Jess replied. "I saw him with it, and it didn't exactly look his speed. I asked; he gave me a hard time." She smiled sweetly. "I figured I'd give it back."

Caitlin grinned. "I like how you think."

She grabbed it out of the storage room, then let Lexi finish ringing up Jess's purchase.

Package in hand, Jess took a step toward the door, then paused and caught Caitlin's eye. "He's actually going to love this book," she said.

Caitlin swallowed the surge of memories that followed. *Don't go there.* "I hope things are going well for him with the new job," she finally said. She managed to spit out the words without her voice breaking. That was something.

Jess frowned. "I probably shouldn't tell you this, but I've never heard him sound more miserable. I thought leaving to chase a ghost was the dumbest thing he'd ever done, but he managed to outdo himself when he walked away from you."

Oh hell. Now she was going to cry, but for what? She'd tried. He'd walked. Discussion over. "I don't know what he told you—"

Jess offered a reassuring smile. "Nothing. But I've known him my entire life. He used to light up when he talked about the department. Now, that's all you."

"He left," Caitlin said. She managed to keep her voice even, but the sharp edges of her emotions left her raw and twisted inside. Again.

"He and his pride will figure it out soon enough, but you didn't hear that from me." Jess glanced around the store. "I'm glad to see so many people supporting you. This place is a sentimental favorite around town. I think you'll be really happy here."

"Thanks," Caitlin said.

Jess nodded and made her way to the door, stopping to greet a couple of people on her way out.

"For what it's worth," Lexi said after Jess left, "I agree with her. He really is an idiot to have walked away from you."

Caitlin tried not to scowl, but keeping her mouth from twisting into a frown took an enormous amount of effort. She didn't disagree. But Shane had followed his heart and ended up in Denver. She'd followed hers and landed in Dry Rock. There wasn't a compromise there, so the fact she was irritated only irritated her more.

Put on your big girl panties and shake it off.

"Well, maybe he's not the only one who needs convincing." Caitlin pocketed her phone. "Can you watch the store for a few minutes?" There was no point in her sitting there glaring at the walls. Not when she could close the book on her so-called relationship with Shane, at least as far as she was concerned.

"Um, sure. Where are you going?"

"To take a selfie."

Chapter Nineteen

Bravado was great in theory.

In the face of a hulking, vibrating bridge, it morphed into a bad idea.

A really, really bad idea.

Caitlin hesitated at the foot of the cross-town bridge, convinced she already felt the span shaking under the weight of the traffic. Why couldn't she have found a bookstore for sale in the desert? With her luck, it would have been at the edge of the Grand Canyon.

Though even that might be preferable to this.

"Breathe," she told herself. "One foot in front of the other. You're too short to be blown over the edge."

At least her bridge-panicked mumbling had been upgraded to a pep talk, however pathetic. Plus, she wasn't crying. Definitely progress. Just a few more steps and she could consider herself on the bridge. After that, it was a matter of taking a selfie without dropping her phone, then sending it to Shane. He'd announced to the world that he was over her by leaving. This would be her version of that. She didn't need his help. Or him.

She needed him to know that.

Maybe she needed to know it, too.

She stared at the bridge, mere steps in front of her. The stupid pedestrian lane offered an impossible choice: cling to the rail that separated her from falling to her death, or skirt the edge of traffic, where massive trucks could roll over her without feeling the bump.

Hero, her ass.

Like it had been a feat to convince her off this thing.

Getting her *on* it, however…

Her slow-motion progress, now all of six inches from dry land, ground to a halt. He *had* gotten her on the bridge. But it didn't count. She was doing this to prove she didn't need him in her life. Totally different thing.

Irritated, she took another step. Then another. It was probably the slowest water crossing since Columbus, but she was doing it.

Without him.

Inch by inch, she forced herself to take each terrifying step, convinced the undulating span had nothing on Tacoma Narrows. The worst part was trying to look normal, or at least the exact opposite of whatever had made someone call her in as a jumper that first day. *All* she needed was for that scenario to play out a second time. Granted, Shane wouldn't be there—as far as she knew, he was off searching for the kind of meaning that required fifty-six floors of concrete instead of twelve. But she didn't need a do-over any more than she needed to offer the guys a second round of ammo.

After nearly thirty painstaking minutes, she neared the center. Above the bridge, a sign announced the name of the river, so she took her first selfie with that in the background, pretty damn proud of herself for not looking terrified. Then she turned to take the hard one—the one where she had to hold the phone up to see the river behind her and far below. Her hand shook so hard she almost dropped the device, but she finally managed to get a somewhat clear shot. She sent them both to Shane via text message. The pictures said what words couldn't: she was moving on.

Satisfied that she'd accomplished something earth-shattering, she crammed the phone in her pocket then eyed the remaining distance. Actually crossing the bridge would be huge, but that would put her on the wrong side of her grand opening, and besides…she was almost halfway. The trip back counted.

If she made it.

She'd make it.

When she turned to head back, a shadow crossed her periphery, but she didn't follow it. Instead, she pinned her eyes on the solid ground ahead and took her first tentative step toward freedom.

And hit a wall that was decidedly *not* in Denver. One whose achingly familiar scent nearly crushed her. Her pulse fluttered, dizzying her, but she'd dropped to her knees for the last time. At least for Lt. Shane Hendricks, or whatever he was now that he'd switched departments.

"You need to move," she told him, trying to ignore the unruly cadence of her heart. There was no denying the shift, or how little it had to do with the bridge.

"Actually, I don't." There he went, straight back to cocky, and barely glancing up from his phone, the jerk. Then she remembered the pictures she'd sent. At least he now had proof they weren't Photoshopped.

"I know I'm short," she told him through gritted teeth, "and I know you have the upper hand, but I swear to God if you don't get out of my way, you'll be on the evening news with me." She paused. "Why are you even here? Aren't you in the wrong city?"

He leaned over the rail, his forearms resting on the top while his shoulders and head extended over the river. "I was."

Caitlin felt sick at the sight of him bent over the railing like that. "Good for you for getting out."

He loosely touched his fingertips and stared down at the water. "That's kind of what I was thinking. In fact, I was on my way back to your grand opening—"

"You're at the wrong address," Caitlin told him. So what if she melted a little because he'd bothered to be there? Her emotions had been raw since the day she'd met him on that bridge. Every girl had her breaking point. "I appreciate the effort, but really, you should go home."

He cocked a brow. "I did."

Whatever that meant. She tried not to stare, but it was either him or the ground, or the river beyond it, and she couldn't go there. Instead, she decided to drown her own way, by looking into his eyes.

"Funny thing about Dry Rock," he said.

She silently willed him to step aside so she could get off that bridge. Her discomfort welled. She didn't dare step into traffic to go around him, and getting past him would require climbing over or under. No way in hell she was getting any higher or crawling, which left only one option: spinning on her heel and heading in the other direction. She'd get a ride back once her feet hit solid ground.

"My family is here," he called after her. "My *life* is here."

"Happy for you," she muttered, probably not anything he heard over the traffic, especially with her back to him.

"My girl is here."

She halted. Turned slowly. He stood several feet away, right where she left him. When she realized the distance she'd traveled without a second thought, pride bubbled in her chest. "*Your girl?*"

"Yes. A pain in my ass redhead with a store full of sex

books."

"No librarian jokes?" she stammered. Really, she had to be hearing him wrong. And if she wasn't, she needed to do something other than swoon, because he didn't deserve it. Not the way he'd left. And what was he going to do? Ambush her at her store?

"Sweetheart, when you knelt in front of me with that little skirt and those glasses and your hair pulled back—"

A passing car honked. Caitlin desperately hoped it was coincidental timing. "You do realize your so-called girl said she was falling in love with you, and you *left*?"

He closed the distance between them. She was grateful he'd finally given up hanging over the edge, but she didn't need him in her face, either. "I waited twenty years for that job, Caitlin. Ten as an adult, but all those dreams before that time counted, too."

She eyed the railing. She *might* be able to get past him… nope, not that brave yet. He watched her, probably waiting for her to fall at his feet and swoon. Hell, she was tempted to do exactly that. He looked too good, and she'd *really* missed him, but they were over. She had to remember that. She *really* needed to get back to solid ground. "You're right," she said. "Those dreams counted. I shouldn't have implied otherwise."

He blinked, and she took advantage of the moment to push past him. For three terror-filled seconds, she had to squeeze against the railing, but then she was free. Nothing but open space between her and her store. She'd been gone so long Lexi was probably losing her shit. Either that, or giving tours of the back room where the sex books were.

Shane didn't try to stop Caitlin, at least not physically. But she was only a few steps into her escape when she realized traffic was no longer whizzing past. She turned to see him standing in the middle of the road, a line of cars stopped behind him. "Yeah, you should have," he said, like he wasn't blocking two lanes of traffic. "Because there's something that matters more."

"You're crazy," she said.

"Kind of like when you showed up at the station and said you were falling in love with me?"

"Yes. And it didn't work out." God help her if the windows were down in any of those cars. Was holding the bridge-goers hostage something that was supposed to work on her?

"I think it could work out," he said.

They really should be having this conversation anywhere else, but that didn't stop her from staring. Of course, there were dozens of people watching him, listening when he called out to her. He tilted his head and shoved his hands in his pockets. "I figured as long as you're in Dry Rock, Denver has nothing on it. Hell, I checked. They haven't had a call for a bridge jumper in months." He approached, slowly, but didn't let the traffic through. "Not once in the last twelve months has a woman smoked herself out of her bookstore trying to use an air conditioner."

Damn it. The knot in her chest loosened.

"No one has reported any kind of rooftop break-ins involving phallic glazed ham-and-Swiss and wine."

"You told me you had permission to be there," she sputtered.

"And now I'm here," he said, "to tell you I love you."

A handful of hoots erupted from the stopped cars. Ordinarily, she might have been mortified, but *ordinarily*, she didn't have a man blocking traffic to say he loved her. He left the road, meeting her where she stood on the side, so close that she could see the hazel in his eyes.

"I love you," he said. He touched the back of her head, tentatively at first, then pulled her in when she didn't resist. And how could she? He was reeling her in, just like he'd always been able to do. "The elevators in Denver," he said, leaning to brush his lips against hers. "They all seem to be working just fine."

"I don't believe that last one," she told him.

"Maybe not," he admitted, "but I was going for a thing."

"Which is?"

"All the excitement I could ever want is here. With you. If you'll have me."

"You left," she said quietly.

"I did," he said, matching her tone. "And that means you won't ever have to wonder what I gave up for you. It wasn't right for me, Caitlin. Not with you here. This thing between us, it's worth fighting for."

Her frustration fled in the wake of his words. No way he'd come back to throw anything insincere at her, but if ever she needed to *not* melt, it was now.

Melting now was the worst thing ever.

"I love you, too," she told him, "but under one condition."

"Anything," he said.

"Scoot over so I can get off this bridge."

Epilogue

Eight months later

Caitlin had to be the only person she knew to have ever twice found herself on a bridge surrounded by emergency responders.

She could only hope this time ended as well as the last.

Butterflies rioted in her chest. A breeze rustled her gown. She couldn't help but feel self-conscious, but how many brides traded the center aisle of a church for a closed-off lane of traffic in the center of the cross-town bridge?

They'd had to promise the ceremony would be quick. At the time, she hadn't wanted to rush her wedding. Now that she was back on the little engineering marvel that had started it all, rushing seemed like the best idea ever had by anyone.

"You okay?" Shane asked.

"Hanging in there," she told him. "But at least this time it's not the bridge stopping my heart." All those nerves...it was because of him. Not because she thought he was going anywhere, but because he was hers, and the enormity of that had no chance of sinking in. In fact, she hoped it never would, because it wasn't something she wanted to take for granted.

"If you have a thing against me dragging you onto bridges, we'll have to come up with a suitable punishment."

She adjusted her dress, hoping the highway grit wouldn't stain the hem. "You keep it up and we'll see."

"I think this was *your* idea," he said.

And not a terrible one. The day was gorgeous. So was her soon-to-be husband. Their families were there, happy and acting like old friends. Everything was perfect, including the fact that they were suspended over a river raging several feet below.

"I made a joking suggestion," she reminded him, "never dreaming they'd actually shut down traffic." Again. It was the third time traffic had stopped for her on this bridge, not that she was counting, but only the second time paramedics were in attendance. She called that progress.

"That's what you get when you marry a man who knows how to make things happen." He wound his fingers through hers, this stolen moment before a wedding she wouldn't have imagined eight months ago. "I love you, Caitlin."

"I'm pretty sure I love you more," she told him. When he gave her a questioning look, she explained, "I'm on a bridge."

He grinned. "You are. And you're beautiful, and you're mine, and I've never wanted anything more." He punctuated the words with a kiss totally worth stopping traffic for.

And this time, she didn't care who saw.

Acknowledgments

This book would not exist without OMG HEATHER HOWLAND KNOWS MY NAME, who might rue the day she met me, but at least now knows how my husband shops for batteries. (But NOT what he did with them. Ahem.) She was so patient during what had to be a torturous editing process that I'm almost certain the open invitation to lurk in her flowerbed is a trap, but one of these days I'll go anyway because she's freaking HEATHER HOWLAND and working directly with her has been one of the biggest honors of my life. Maybe one day I'll even be able to talk with her on the phone without fangirling, wheezing, and generally embarrassing myself, but don't count on it. Like, ever. Because, erm, she's Heather Howland.

Kira-Archer-slash-Michelle-McLean, my #creepytwin, I have no idea how I'd get through a single word without you. Writing is a solitary existence, but having you there has made it feel like a years-long slumber party. Plus, you don't touch my rum, so we're beyond cool. (Until I break out the spiders, but they're just little things. Besides which, revenge has been had. *shudder*)

My family… We've been through this over twenty times now, and you're still speaking to me. Which I love and appreciate, though also suspect when I'm down to the wire on a deadline, you're all happier when I disappear to write. (Y'all didn't know I'd figured that out, did you?) Thanks for tolerating me through the worst of it.

Ryan, you're the best part of every hero I write. (And you make them all look bad, so thanks for that.)

For my readers, and in particular the members of my street team, your support means the world to me. I wouldn't be here without you.

And finally, a special shout out to Heather-from-Maine, whose stories of horrifyingly awkward moments have kept me in hysterics. I'm so glad to give you a heroine to whom you can *really* relate. Now excuse me while I back away before any of this rubs off on me. (Just kidding. I'll see you on release day…but don't touch my rum.)

About the Author

Sarah and her husband of what he calls "many long, long years" live on the mid-Atlantic coast with their six young children, all of whom are perfectly adorable when they're asleep. She never dreamed of becoming an author, but as a homeschooling mom, she often jokes she writes fiction because if she wants anyone to listen to her, she has to make them up. (As it turns out, her characters aren't much better than the kids.) When not buried under piles of laundry, she may be found adrift in the Atlantic (preferably on a boat) or seeking that ever-elusive perfect writing spot where not even the kids can find her.

She loves creating unforgettable stories while putting her characters through an unkind amount of torture—a hobby that has nothing to do with living with six children. (Really.) Though she adores sexy contemporary romance, Sarah writes in many genres including historical and ghostly supernatural romance and romantic suspense. Her ever-growing roster of releases may be found on Amazon, Barnes & Noble, Kobo, iBooks, Google Books, and Entangled Publishing.

Find love in unexpected places with these satisfying Lovestruck reads…

Ten Days with the Highlander
a *Love Abroad* novel by Hayson Manning

There's no way Callum MacGregor is going to let a gorgeous American turn his hotel in the Scottish Highlands over to bored tourists looking to satisfy their *Outlander* fantasies. But if he can get go-getter Georgia Paxton to slow down and see the magic of the town and its people, maybe he won't have to run her out of the county…or his heart.

The Hook Up
a *First Impressions* novel by Tawna Fenske

Content with her booming career as a purveyor of Madame Butterfly pleasure aids, Ellie Sanders doesn't need a man for anything—except maybe marketing tips. And, okay, a few fun nights with something that doesn't require batteries. Enter Tyler Hendrix. The Navy helped Ty put his tumultuous childhood behind him, but when sexy single mom Ellie walks through the First Impressions door looking for a way to take her business to the next level, their scorching sexual attraction threatens to crumble Tyler's walls for good…

In a Ranger's Arms
a *Men of At Ease Ranch* novel by Donna Michaels

Former Army Ranger Stone Mitchum doesn't have time for sex. He's too busy running a construction company and transitioning veterans back into society, but when Jovy Larson falls into his arms, his libido snaps to attention. To prove she worthy of taking over her family's company, she's trying to sell gluten-free, vegan food—in the middle of cattle country, Texas. But by the time her lease runs out and the test is over, she's faced with a new challenge…competing against Stone's sense of duty to win his heart.

Driven to Temptation
a novel by Melia Alexander

Aidan Ross might be an engineering genius, but people skills? Not this soldier's forte. Thankfully, a trusted friend is accompanying him to a make-or-break tradeshow…but then a bubbly redhead hops into his truck, claiming to be his new road trip buddy. She's a gorgeous distraction he can't afford. Or ignore.

Made in the USA
Middletown, DE
12 August 2020